ORANGES FOR THE SON OF
ALEXANDER LEVY

AF

BIELSKI, NELLA
ORANGES FOR THE SON OF ALEXANDER LEVY

DATE DUE

OCT. 1 8 1988		
NOV. 1 1988		
R 11-15-88		
JUL 0 7 1997		

Oranges for the Son of Alexander Levy

NELLA BIELSKI

Writers and Readers Publishing Cooperative Society Ltd.
144 Camden High Street, London NW1 0NE England

First published in French by Mercure de France 1979
Published by
Writers and Readers Publishing Cooperative 1982

Cover Design Chris Hyde

Photoset by Photobooks (Bristol) Limited
Barton Manor, St. Philips, Bristol
Printed and bound by Billings Ltd, Guildford, Worcester and
London

ISBN 0 906495 70 9

'Writers and Readers gratefully acknowledge the assistance of
the Arts Council of Great Britain in the translation of this book.'

To My Mother

I no longer knew where I was with Paul. He was living, without pretending otherwise, with another woman. Mother Xenia was dying. The night before I had mashed a banana with some cream cheese for her. She was lying back against her pillow. Everything tired her these days, lying, sitting, eating, not eating. Twice a day they gave her injections. I don't know of what. Something which helped her to keep going.

She kept going. For the last three years, that's what I had done too. First I kept going for days, then for months, then through the seasons. Let's stop there with the seasons. I kept going, that's all. The previous autumn had not been so bad. That's when I had the courage to throw Paul out. There was no longer any reason for not finishing with the whole affair. But this only accounted for one autumn.

Mother was dying. It was winter, February, and Mother was going to be dead by the fourth of March. I was going to hear the news in Gif sur Yvette in the Ile de France. Now I

1

was in Moscow for ten days. I slept at the Hotel Metropole or at the house of some friends in Herzen Street. Each morning I took a taxi to Zelenograd, the green belt city, forty kilometres away. Mother had rented a new flat there to die in. I had never seen this flat before. It was not home. Of my home all that was left were my mother and Aunt Tanya— Aunt Tanya who has been good during all the seventy years of her life and who comes from the Ukraine. It was she who announced to Mother that her third new-born child had sexual parts in the shape of a half-moon. So, in a way, it was still home, with these two women there, the one who had conceived me and carried me inside her, and the one who had seen me come out. If I insist on these first facts so much, it's because I'm no longer living with Paul. Otherwise, I'd think it exaggerated.

Now that Paul is sleeping with somebody else, under another roof, the whole question of home has become important to me. So my mother's new flat in the glass city, which wasn't my home, became my home simply because it contained the two people in the world who were closest to me, not counting Pauline and Paul. I don't believe a home is a question of walls.

For the first seven mornings I found Mother there in the new flat waiting for me with her usual patience. On the eighth morning I arrived and she was no longer there. Aunt Tanya opened the door to me. The second door, the one into Mother's room was closed, presumably in order not to shock me. That's so like my Aunt: as if the few seconds of being protected from what I was about to discover could change something. During the night Mother had vomited bananas, cream cheese and then blood, a lot of blood. At dawn they had taken her off to hospital. In socialist countries emergencies are dealt with quickly. For me, in the space of those few seconds, which Aunt Tanya had wanted to give me by keeping the door shut, Mother died.

Zelenograd is all mirrors and open spaces. You cross it by bus. The streets, as in New York, have numbers instead of names. This

3

makes a difference. No more addresses commemorating the Red Army, or the 25th of October, or Lenin. The numbers of the buildings, for no apparent reason, are astronomically high. A kind of architectural space-fiction, reminding me of some of the Saturday-afternoon-films on television which Pauline watches, lying on the floor, far away in France.

In a pine forest at the edge of the city, we come to a hospital which is as white as virgin snow. This is where I'm supposed to find what is left to me of Xenia who is vomiting blood. I leave my Aunt and my sister-in-law at the door. For someone so gravely ill, only one person has the right to visit; and today this person is Xenia's daughter, who has come thousands of miles from Paris to see her.

I take off my coat, my boots, my scarf. I slip on some white canvas boots over my tights. Clutching my handbag which is too big, and in which I carry all my treasures, I climb up to the fifth floor and enter room 569. There are four beds. And there is Mother, not far from

4

the door, her two arms attached to drips for serum and blood. By her lips, I can see that she's speaking to me, but I can't hear her. I move my ear closer. 'My adorable little doll,' she manages to say. Straight away I start to cry, despite all the promises I have made to myself. For my weakness, I blame Paul or perhaps this snarling bitch of a life. That Mother, in the state she was, should say such sweet things was too much. 'Take care of Paul,' she adds softly, 'and do up that button.' I do up the shirt button which her eyes indicate.

About Paul, I keep quiet. I tell her nothing about Paul. Because he's Paul, he's always there, like Pauline. Paul—Pauline—Liola. Mother used to say that we three, the trio of us, were her greatest joy on earth. I wanted to keep this intact for her. Not a word, not even a whisper. I turn my eyes away and dab at my tears, tears which have been so rare the last three years. Crying was something I un-learned, thanks to Paul.

Clear-sighted now, I look only at the blood-stained dressing around her elbow and at her white face on the flat pillow. Her face is still alive, it moves, it lifts itself up and changes its angle on the flat pillow. Mother never liked flat pillows. In bed she usually had two, three, several pillows, and never flat ones, they were always puffed up. Four taps with the back of her hand and she had a pillow puffed up. And I learnt to do the same. Economic gestures are one of the things she has bequeathed to me. These gestures have become like prayers. I cut onions like her, roll out pastry like her, I get pleasure like her from watching people eat.

She wasn't really there that day, she was leaving, moving away towards death, very quickly and all-too-clearly. I was to stay behind, holding the life-line. I was strengthened a little by the fact that—in her eyes at least—I was strong enough to do this. To me, it was less clear. I felt myself slipping away, drop by drop, with the blood she was losing. I was dying too and the blood I was losing was Paul. Paul, who was still interminably leaving

6

me. It's strange how long some people take to leave you.

In fact I'm not sure whether I was thinking of Paul as I watched Mother struggling to live. She was dying. Paul had nothing to do with it, nor did Pauline. On my return I would tell Pauline nothing about the agony Mother was suffering. Pauline with her freckles and turned-up nose was eleven years old, but she had lived through the last stage with Paul in utter panic. Why do I bring everything back to Paul? It's unnecessary. Sitting in the chair, looking at Mother and the snow and the pine trees through the large window with scarlet curtains, a tap dripping somewhere behind me, and the blood-stained rag around Mother's arm, I nonetheless return to Paul without really meaning to.

One day Pauline will be sitting here, Pauline married, already a mother. It will be my turn to leave. She will be looking at me as I am now looking at Mother. That idea has for me something wonderfully normal about it. It is astonishing how much I love the normal.

7

The spring comes after winter. Christmas comes regardless of what one does. It is a certainty. And this is what I love. I dampen a handkerchief and wet Mother's lips with it. She is not allowed to drink.

Mother isn't complaining, which is hardly surprising given all the drugs they have pumped into her. But her strength is so much on the wane that it must be painful. Not even to have the strength to suffer, to regret, to get into a rage—that is a sure sign of a life on the ebb. That much I know.

Paul had managed to make me understand that he lived only for one woman, and that woman wasn't me. He had succeeded in doing this by writing. When he puts his mind to it, Paul writes better than anyone else.

I see myself on the landing of the house at Gif. Pauline was at school. I was beginning to cut up a bedcover, a bedcover of white cotton circles crocheted together, which Mother had given me. It was a masterpiece. And I was cutting it up, destroying it, white circle by white circle, with the same intensity as

8

Mother had put into the making of it. I was mad with pain and I had almost nothing to hold on to. Here, face to face with Mother, I certainly have something to hold on to.

One year, just one short year after the day on the landing with the bedcover, I was walking with a man beside the railings of the Luxembourg Gardens. It was autumn and everywhere there were dead leaves. In my last novel there had been a similar scene: a man and a woman, Jeanne and Alexander, walking beside the railings of the Summer Gardens in Petersburg. I wanted to write more about how happy my Jeanne was to be doing just that, just walking and scuffling the dry leaves. But I told myself: Liola, forget it! The dead leaves, the park railings, it's a bit too much, isn't it?

Suddenly now those other kind of leaves, the leaves of typing paper which I had thrown into the wastepaper basket were blown back to me. At my feet were the dead leaves of the trees in the Luxembourg Gardens, and beside me there were a man's blue eyes under a cap.

9

Everything in me awoke. I was at home again in time; I could remember things.

On the day of the bedcover, time had ceased to exist for me, I felt it no more than I felt anything else. Kostia, the man with the cap, was carrying a case full of manuscripts which he hesitated to publish in Moscow. As for me, I was incapable of writing any more. Censorship, prohibitions, obstacles, they come in different guises.

I collect all these obstacles and look at them, and place them like pebbles by the side of the road, just like in the story of Tom Thumb. When I do not know how to go on, I can see all the pebbles along the way I've come. It's over Paul that I stumble most. Yet time and again the very act of stumbling brings me back to life, reminding me of the blood and the salt which flows through our veins and which will go on doing so for as long as we live. The salt which is free to choose, which flows or which hardens, and which holds us together.

The bottle of blood was emptying itself and

10

this was a proof that Mother was alive. Her face, anyway, was less pale than the night before. Even in her old age Mother had a smooth skin with freckles like Pauline. What wrinkles faces, I think, is spitefulness, intolerances, jealousy, the desire to possess, a lack of goodness. I'm not thinking of the ordinary wrinkles of the skin, but of ravaged faces, faces whose expression and spirit are like a ruin.

When I was little I was always losing my ribbons, they slipped out of my too fine, too straight hair. This complicated Mother's budget. She used to scold me too about my gloves, I was always losing one glove and then the other was useless. About my scarves too, which I left everywhere. Later she used to scold me about my trousers. Even when it was cold, I refused to wear them. The trousers had to be seen to be believed. They transformed you into a shapeless woollen doll, like the kind you put over a teapot to keep it warm.

Finally I had to put on the trousers since Mother couldn't be argued with on this point.

11

But no sooner out of the door, than I hid them under the cellar stairs. One day the cellar got flooded and the trousers disappeared, they were carried away by the current. That was a memorable day, not one of my happier ones. I can understand Mother now: it was no joke trying to find a warm garment in the shops during a socialist winter.

I can't bring myself to scold Pauline when she treats her clothes just as badly as I did. She loses and dirties her clothes as easily as she breathes. She comes in with a pair of jeans hopelessly torn and then it's I who have to console *her*. Her tears encourage mine and we both end up by crying.

But since Paul left the house in Gif, I never cry openly. Paul says that when he first knew me in Moscow, I used to cry in trams, in parks, in railway stations, in swimming pools, in telephone booths, museums, aeroplanes, corridors. He is exaggerating as usual—it's one of his charms.

Paul and I met in Moscow a long time ago. I was wearing a dress that Mother had made for

12

me out of a remnant—it was blue with little white flowers—which had probably been intended for something like a pillow case. Not at all smart, yet I liked it very much. It was the month of July. At five o'clock every morning, I left home to travel sixty kilometres, first by train and then by bus. My brother, Genia, had found me a job and this earned me a few hundred roubles a month. The money was going to stop Mother worrying. She was worried because in the autumn I was going into my fourth year at the philosophy faculty and I had no shoes. There was also the problem of a winter coat. The winter before, she had managed to get the padding and the lining; now it was a question of buying the cloth itself.

That summer I used to carry a book by a Belgian philosopher in a string bag. I had to review it for *Problems of Philosophy*. In the train and in the bus, I slept sitting up. I was getting nowhere with the book. On the construction site, where my brother was manager, my job was to note down all the workers present and

13

absent. Then I slept standing up. Sometimes I used to go and sleep, stretched out in the Ostankino Park near the building site; it was a way of profitting from the weaknesses of the socialist economy. Then came the lunch break. Usually I went to have whatever was on the day's menu, and a glass of tea, in the Ostankino Restaurant. That's where I saw Paul for the first time, or, more accurately, where Paul saw me. From the day of my birth I've been as short-sighted as a mole, and up till then I refused to wear glasses, preferring to live in a haze.

I get up to adjust Mother's arm, it has fallen off the edge of the bed. By accident, my elbow rubs against her chest and it hurts her as much as if I had hit her. Even the thin blanket of this over-heated hospital is an intolerable weight for her. The drug is wearing off, the injection isn't working any more. I go into the hall to find a nurse. I empty the chamber pot which also has mucus and blood in it. We all contain litres of blood, normally we don't think about it, we are only aware of it when we're

14

losing it, when we are losing blood or love.

Mother asks me to cover her. She has had another injection. I make the gesture of tucking her in, just as I do at Gif in the evenings for Pauline. Mother doesn't like it. In Russia you never tuck the sheet under the mattress. It's left loose and you roll yourself up in it. I was forgetting.

Seeing Mother refuse the tucked-in sheet, I remember how I instinctively rediscovered that way of rolling yourself in, of swaddling yourself in the bedclothes, as soon as Paul had gone for good from my bed. This made me think about Paul's warmth again. Even now, in the debris of the shipwreck which he so carefully organized, it's impossible for me to deny Paul's warmth; that warmth which was part of my very first impression of him.

I was finishing a cutlet in the Ostankino Restaurant. I could hazily make out some ten people sitting at a reserved table. Right in the middle of the table there was a red, white and blue flag on a miniature flagpole, planted in an iron stand. Frenchmen. All of them were

15

intent on reading the menus from top to bottom, those menus which promise everything that the culinary art of communism might produce if imagination and science were combined. The choice ranged from octopus in sea-kale to partridge in bilberries, passing by the famous 'Kasha Gourieff'. So many extinct gastronomical species! I knew very well that those menus were a form of epitaph, a purely verbal homage to pre-1913 Russian cuisine. Yet peering at the poor famished Frenchmen, I told myself that perhaps, just for them, a miracle would be produced.

The waitress came to take their orders, and firmly announced that no attention whatsoever should be paid to what was printed—that was literature. The eatable food, the available food, was listed on a little piece of loose paper attached to the cover of the menu with a clip.

I had the impression that the Frenchmen had taken in the bad news, but that in order to amuse themselves a little, they were pretending not to understand so that the waitress

16

would have to repeat her speech all over again. She was out of her depth. That's when I intervened. Perhaps I used a somewhat peculiar French, influenced by my Belgian philosopher's thinking about Hegel. Anyway, I provoked an outburst of laughter such as I had never heard or seen in sober adults. They were choking. Savages! Under Stalin we had lost the habit of such scenes of impropriety in public places!

I paid my bill and was drinking my last sip of tea, when suddenly the little circle of Frenchmen, calm now, approached my table. I particularly noticed a man with badly cut black hair, a blue mediterranean fisherman's sweater and crumpled trousers. He bowed, took my hand and kissed it, as if we were in Madame de Guermantes' velvet drawing room. Nonplussed, I just had time to notice a few white hairs at his temples and a network of fine wrinkles near his eyes. Nobody kisses your hand in the Soviet Union and I could easily have found his gesture vulgar. I let it pass, perhaps because of those little signs of a man getting on in age. No, let me be frank—it had more to do with the fact that somehow this man intrigued me. I could feel in him something that was both highly-strung and calm, something unusual which wasn't simply to be explained by the fact that he was from a different country. From the start, I felt that there might be a kinship between this stranger and myself.

I got up in my pillow-case dress, walked away and no longer gave the matter much thought. But at home in Kuntsevo that evening, while I was reading a new chapter on Hegel with the help of a dictionary, this stranger came back to me in a flash. Quickly I shut both my eyes and the dictionary, and I asked a secret question—Russian schoolgirls often do this. My eyes still closed, I opened the dictionary at random and let a finger land on the page. I opened my eyes to read the answer. To the left of my fingernail was the word 'Marriage'.

It wasn't a good summer for me. I had wanted to go to the Black Sea, but the problem of my coat and shoes kept me to my building site. It was a cushy job, thanks to my brother Genia, but due to a lack of sleep, I felt too tired even to go to the Film Festival in Moscow, although I was mad about the cinema. Mother even thought that my nose was growing pinched—and this wasn't a good sign. Mother always paid a great deal of attention to the nose. For her it was a gauge of whether or not I was wasting away.

Now I am looking at Mother's nose and her sleeping face on the flat pillow. For somebody who has so little time before them, perhaps it is sad to sleep. Paul left behind in the house—on purpose or did he forget it?—a book on cancer which describes various methods of euthanasia. The most advanced and progressive methods. When the suffering is too much and there is no hope left, they kill you very gently: they inject you with cocktails which send you to sleep deliciously and forever. Some people don't like to be put to sleep in this way, especially children. They are the ones who fight most fiercely against going. As if they knew that sleep has certain advantages over being awake, but only on condition that waking is guaranteed.

When Mother wasn't sleeping, she called for sleep, and when she felt sleep coming, she protested. And she protested so faintly that it hurt me, because, until then, she had always made what she wanted very clear, she always knew how to give orders and take command.

When, during the war, we left Moscow to go as refugees to a small lost village at the foot of the Urals, she saw to it that we took warm things with us: felt boots, duvets, thick coats. Her friends who were officer's wives, her Moscovite friends, did not think of taking anything except their fox furs and their crêpe de Chine dresses. And this made life difficult for them in a village where every morning you had to break snow with a shovel just to get out the door. It was a village of women and children, like us the ones from Moscow, and the ones who had always lived there. The men from the Moscow families and the men from the village families were all at the war. My father was at the Volkhov front near Leningrad.

During the time we spent in this village I retained three images from the past: an image of an ordinary orange, an image of a kind of ice cream which you put into a mould and it comes out rectangular between two wafers, and the image of a little bar of chocolate wrapped in silver paper. Image is the right word. I had forgotten the tastes. The time passed slowly. I spent hours sitting on the stove next to a very old man. He was the only grown-up member of the family where we were billetted. The rest of the family were ten or twelve years old, the age of my two brothers. This family of temporary orphans shared their new frozen potatoes with us. These potatoes were slightly sweet, not very good. I used to eat them with my mind's eye fixed on my three images: the orange, the ice cream and the chocolate.

These imaginary meals would then lead to another vision: that of the war being over. Men were coming home, above all my father

21

was coming home. In his arms he was holding the doll of my dreams: a plastic baby that I could bath. In the Moscow streets there were ice cream kiosks, coloured balloons. This vision of mine was distinguished by the total absence of snow, as if victory on the battle fields would bring in its train a complete change of weather. Confidence in this final victory was shared by both the peasants and the townswomen who were continually coming to our house.

Mother knew how to read cards like no one else on that side of the Urals. She also knew, when necessary, exactly how to cover up her mistakes. She could cover up with anything. When her talents were rewarded, we had two or three eggs to go with our potatoes or sometimes even a tiny scrap of bacon. This happened above all when Mother predicted a leave and the man in question then came home. Came home not in a dream, but by road, having travelled a long way. Really came home. It didn't matter if he wasn't always a complete man—a limb or some other

22

part might be missing—but it was still him. In the village all the women were waiting for their men, whole or not.

I was waiting for mine. I was already one of the women. I waited with such longing that he finally came, without his right arm but with my doll. Later Mother told me that I hid under the bed, Father couldn't get me out, I shouted that I didn't love him any more. And then—as was bound to happen—I left my place under the bed, left the warmth of the stove and spent days and nights on his knees. He had both knees. I don't want to draw any comparisons between childhood and maturity on the subject of how the man you love is absent and then returns. I'd rather believe that one can always keep a certain presence of mind.

At last the war ended and, as in my dreams, the snow did melt. Though it came back. We were in Moscow, Father was there. I remember the whole sky. It was as multi-coloured as a rainbow and even more beautiful. There were rockets of every kind, as if all the world's flowers had met in the sky. I was perched on Father's shoulders and I was licking a strawberry ice cream. I watched the German prisoners file by. I learnt later that this idea of having them file past us like trapped animals was Stalin's. They weren't at all as I had imagined. They were ashen and in rags. I felt a great shame; my father said nothing. The crowd stood there amazed and silent and you could hear the muffled plodding of thousands of bare or bandaged feet.

Mother bequeathed me her round nose. All the rest of me is Father's. The nose is frivolous, up in the air. Tonight as I watch her sleeping on the flat pillow, Mother's nose has effectively grown longer, as if pinched. Death is already doing his work, modelling her nose in his own image. She always had small hands, now they are even smaller, for she has grown so thin during the last year. One of her arms lies across her chest. The other arm would be there too if it weren't held to one side by the drip. When I go to sleep without Paul, I cross my arms over my chest as though I were

24

embracing myself. What time can it be? In the ward only a night light is burning. I'm not sleepy.

Vladimir Petrovitch, the surgeon on duty, told me this morning that he would come and take me away for a moment, that we could have tea together. When? He didn't know. It depended upon the condition of a patient he was about to operate on. He told me that my idea of spending the night here with my mother was not very clever; and that, in any case, it was not allowed. "Just one night, Vladimir Petrovitch, one short night, the last one."

He listened without listening, as if he had foreseen what I was going to say. As he walked away, he said, "If I may, I'll come and find you tonight." My country is like that. People spend their lives getting round what is forbidden.

Mother used to make my dresses, as she did everything I wore. A little surprisingly, she always wanted my dresses to mould my hips. She saw no harm in that. At least that's the way it was from the day I had any hips. The line of her life and my hips were somehow linked.

In the dim light of the single bulb, thoughts come and dance in my head. In my memory I watch one of my own private films of the sixties. Jean-Luc was a friend of Paul's in those days. In the house at Gif I have a photo of Jean-Luc, without his glasses. He is lying on some crumpled sheets, a little as if he were floating on white waves. I often look at this photo. With no glasses, his eyes are melancholy, bewildered. Nothing protects him. When he was struggling with his real films, he used to call me Apple. Then came the year of the Chinoiseries, and he no longer called me Apple because I wasn't Chinese. I think he even held it against me that I wasn't Chinese. One day he came to the house, as usual, without warning. That day Pauline had spilt a large pot of oil paint over her head. I have never quite understood how she did this, because she was scarcely bigger than the heavy paint pot. I spent all the afternoon trying to clean her up with almond oil. There was still paint in her ears, her nose, the corners of her eyes. Not long before, Paul had hidden Pauline under his overcoat and taken her to see *Pierrot le Fou*. So I turned to Jean-Luc and said: 'It's all your fault!'

At that time the cinema was one of Paul's passions and I used to go to films with him. On the pavement, on the side of the Champs Elysées with odd numbers, we met Jean-Luc. His black overcoat made him look very thin, dark glasses protected his eyes, glasses which in the winter night gave him something of the air of a gangster. He scarcely ever unclenched his teeth or laughed, but when he did laugh, it was like a miracle. He liked pasta, cakes and fast silent cars. Once he lent me one of those cars. I shouldn't have taken it, for it exploded half-way up the Boulevard Raspail. Now I no longer know what Jean-Luc likes. He's not around any more. As for Paul's likes and dislikes, insofar as I know them, they leave me cold. I can do nothing about it.

At night faces you have forgotten during

the day come back. I'm no specialist in insomnia. I sleep, regardless, my arms crossed over my chest, still confident that I'm going to wake up. In the past I didn't think about any of this. Life went on of its own accord, quietly. Paul, the night-time, the daytime, Jean-Luc's films, potatoes baked in the oven, Mother and Father telephoning from Moscow asking me to come and see them, Pauline learning to talk, summertime in the little house lent to us by my friend Fenosa in San Vincent in Catalonia. I didn't look for any explanations. What went on inside me barely interested me, I only noticed the gestures and acts of others: Jean-Luc's rare smiles, Sonia's coughing fits which were beginning to get worse in the year of the Chinoiseries, Paul seeing less and less of Jean-Luc, Sonia and I trying to find out why she coughed with such terrible violence when in principle there was nothing the matter with her lungs. Yet life still went on. The tempo of my second book was inevitably that of a waltz. One, two, three! The feet of Jeanne, the heroine, come together in one place on the floor of the dance hall, before being swept away to another.

Nothing comes effortlessly any more. That is finished. In the morning, I insist upon going through the list of my hopes, the full list. But during the course of the day, they get scattered. Day after day I change myself into a soldier who fights for a purpose, who has to invent a sense for things. Going on living is a series of battles, some of which I lose.

On a beach on the Costa Dorada, where I still go for the summers with Pauline, there are some flowers called sand lilies. Delicate and white, these flowers possess a rare insolence. They grow out of the rubbish daily left behind by campers and, on Sundays, by people from Barcelona: they grow through opened, jagged sardine tins, through beer bottles full of sand, through packets of Ducados cigarettes, rotten fruit, plastic bags. The sand lilies are stubborn, they flower, and each summer they are more numerous and more sweetly perfumed.

Fenosa, who was born in the nineteenth

29

century, had a grandfather on his father's side who was a lamplighter. He is a sculptor. His sculptures, called little Fenosas or big Fenosas, as if they were the children and grandchildren of a family, are mostly of women. Fire women, cloud women, sun women, storm women. He takes a little moist clay and makes women for himself. With the tips of his trembling fingers, he caresses the forming shape. Then he takes off the excess clay with a seashell. These figures, like flowers shipped over long distances, are put to sleep in flat boxes. Later they're changed into bronzes so that they will die less soon.

Sometimes it happened that I took hold of some sand lilies and squeezed them tightly, unable to let them go. I brought them back from the beach and placed them in a glass of water in front of Fenosa. They kept us company while we ate salted cod and tomatoes. Fenosa has no sense of thrift except where speech is concerned. I feel happy near him. His eyes are always saying something. So too are his hands, his hair, his soul, his clay

30

women. But out loud, Fenosa says almost nothing. This time, the sand lilies did make him utter more than three words. 'Given the way they've begun, these flowers will go far,' he said. 'Men, trees, birds, will vanish. The world will no longer be habitable for them. Swallows are already disappearing. These days you see only martins flying at dusk and they are stronger, but they too will vanish. Only those flowers, those lilies, will stay. They'll people the planet. They'll build towns with many fountains!'

Fenosa is right. The sand lilies have courage and many talents. Yet near them, on the beach, I once saw a mother looking after her child in a deck chair. He had skeletal legs, the legs of Treblinka. The patience with which the mother constantly moved those legs so that they could benefit from the sun was beyond reason. She believed she could bring them back to life, that one day they would grow muscles and walk like other legs. To me her faith was even stronger than the capacity of the sand lilies to draw up water from the

31

depths of the sand. Her faith was much, much stronger.

I won't admit that Mother is no longer believing me when I tell her that she will see the Spring, and that Pauline will come and visit her. In a similar way, somewhere inside me, I won't admit that I've lost Paul.

It's when I'm ill in bed, when I have a high temperature, that I have the most common sense. I make myself consider the empty space beside me. I say to myself that the space wouldn't be less empty if I were a widow. Does this comfort me? No, it doesn't. And then I tell myself frankly: it is essential in life to learn to endure absences; to prepare oneself for the death of others, for one's own death. A little training so that the big moments of reckoning are not too shocking.

Meanwhile there is still the lilac, its flowers coming through the window, and there is Pauline who comes up the stairs each morning. How does she know that I am so fragile in the morning? She does nothing to upset me, she doesn't even say anything silly which might make me smile. From where did she get this gift?

When I was Pauline's age and had to be woken up to go to school, Mother did all she could to make the shift from night to day easy for me, especially in the winter. I was asleep when she pulled on my stockings. My eyes were still closed when she did my hair. As she put on my knickers, my shirt, my skirt, I gradually found myself in a standing position. And there was my tea waiting. I rubbed my eyes. Mother stirred the spoon in the cup to make the sugar dissolve. She kissed me rarely. Her acts took the place of kisses.

Did Mother believe in God? I asked her one day in Zelenograd. She made a gesture with her hand, a gesture which didn't mean anything at all, and then she looked at the wall. How well I remember one morning, just after the first night when Mother, Paul and I slept in the same room, Mother on her bed, and I with him on the sofa. Paul left for work very early and I began to cry. Mother came and sat next to me, took me in her arms and

33

said, 'It's beautiful when you love one another. The most beautiful thing that can happen to anyone when you love one another.'

Mother had a weakness for Paul. I saw this. The pancakes she made him eat in the morning were particularly inspired. I was well placed to judge. Paul wore neither tie nor suit, not even his overcoat accorded with her ideas. At first she despaired of the fact that he looked like a tramp. Then she accepted it.

When I am writing, it almost seems as if I'm not. I write slowly, just putting one foot in front of the other. I take my time in order to find out. Find out what? I'm somebody who can't be rushed. Pauline knows that. Mother and Father knew it. Yet suddenly on the stairs, Paul turned round and said point blank, 'I'm haunted by the image of a woman I've met. I can't get her out of my mind.'

Somewhere between the age of twelve and sixteen, we go through a woolly period. The wool muffles the world, as if to make the changes taking place in us less painful. The

34

capacity to forget is wonderful then. Pauline, still little, hasn't reached this period yet. But I went through it again, a kind of delayed reaction. If I hadn't, I couldn't have gone on.

Paul took trains, went, came back. He and the woman who haunted him were waiting to love one another openly. I behaved as if all this were the most natural thing in the world. In newspapers, in books, everywhere, there was only the supreme power of Sexual Desire, as celebrated by the analysts. In Paris people were freeing themselves, just as they were in other capitals. And I, a Russian, a provincial in these matters, I tried to escape to somewhere within myself. There I wasn't altogether alone. I made myself work. Jeanne, the young woman in my novel, helped me. She proved her worth. I piled sorrow after sorrow upon her, abandonment after abandonment, to see how she would face up to it all.

I remember I was typing the last pages of a chapter: it was about Russia during the civil war. Jeanne was searching everywhere for Alexander, her man, her lover. A ray of sunshine fell on my back, warming it, and for the first time since Paul had been 'haunted', I had a sense of well-being. It was only a ray of sunshine, nothing to dance about.

I never again want to see Paul dancing in the sunshine at Barcelona airport by the fountain and the giant clock. Sonia was going back to Paris, Paul was arriving the same day at almost the same time. Pauline was there, looking like a peach with her red hair and golden cheeks. Pauline was still young enough to be happy wearing dresses. I was talking with Sonia. She made a sign with her eyes and I turned round to see Paul dancing by the fountain with Pauline in his arms. The sunlight, coming through the airport windows, was streaming down on them.

Yet I was still good for something. I could still go on writing about Jeanne's life, because my other memories vanished before this one of Paul waltzing with Pauline. And another one too: the image of Pauline's face when I saw her for the first time. I had been put to sleep for the caesarean. When I woke

36

up, Pauline was there, wrapped in white, her face framed by a bonnet. She was fresh and rested: caesareans have at least that advantage. For me there can be no face more beautiful than that of Pauline's on her first day of life. Yes, all mothers say this. But I stress it, I think, to reaffirm what belongs to us for ever, our only happiness on this earth, a handful of moments, the waltz by the fountain for example, and Pauline's face on her first day.

For a long time Pauline refused to speak. She was neither deaf nor blind, she had everything she needed and in the right place. I didn't worry. After all, she heard her mother speaking Russian to her friends and Sonia speaking Armenian on the telephone, she heard Spanish and Portuguese being spoken by the young women minding the children in the park, and everything else was said in French. She was a little lost in the midst of all this. At last, one winter night around three or four in the morning, she deigned to speak. She wasn't sleeping and Sonia, who only slept in the daytime for a few hours, was holding Pauline in her arms by the window. Pauline pointed a finger toward the trees and said: 'Someone black.' She said it calmly, intelligibly, thoughtfully, without a trace of a Russian or any other accent, and with nothing childish in her tone.

After this forbidding beginning, her mind focused on prehistoric monsters. Paul brought her picture books full of saurians. Models of dinosaurs, ichthyosaurs and other prehistoric lizard-like animals were her only toys. She spent hours gazing at highly coloured, very lifelike pictures of these creatures: their long slack bodies rising from the mud in the midst of giant flowers, their tiny heads lost in the sky amidst flying reptiles. Once more I am looking over Pauline's shoulder at these creatures and once more I am struck by their gaze. In man and animal everything depends upon the look in the eyes, and in their reconstructions from fossil evidence, the painters of these pictures were able to recreate all the secondary components of these animals, but not the look in their eyes, and so their eyes didn't exist. They were absent eyes. Like the absent look in the eyes of the polio-ridden child on the Catalonian beach; like Mother's eyes when she blankly noticed the bouquet of snowdrops I'd placed on her bedside table; or that look I sometimes catch in Fenosa's eyes when his vocal cords betray him and he can't quite put into words one of his thoughts about the stars.

Leaping in one bound over the entire history of the earth, Pauline passed without any transition from the gaze of the ichthyo-saurus to science fiction. Films like *Close Encounters of the Third Kind* she saw at least ten times. I went with her once. She wanted me to. Clinging grimly to the armrests, she no longer moved or breathed. In the dark, her eyes shone brighter than the stars on the screen. At the climax, when the saucer arrived, they were full of tears. Though I found the giant saucer and its music very beautiful, I did not understand why so many people should suddenly find themselves so involved in the

39

image of a sacred, truncated mountain they had never seen. I told Pauline so. She looked at me indulgently for a long while, then took my hand, made me sit down and talked to me about dreams, intuition, mediums—a whole little course in parapsychology. Sometimes she stopped to ask me whether I understood. Her knowledge impressed me less than the naturalness, without disappointment or contempt, with which she wanted to make good my ignorance.

Doctor Jung says somewhere that the most deeply buried fibres of our psychic life may be vestiges of ancient nervous systems—like those of the lobsters—or of spinal marrow originating millenia ago in the dinosaurs. I think sometimes that this must be what Paul touched in me—these fibres of a primordial past. That might explain why I am unable to forget him or the one who haunts him.

I suddenly woke in the dark and could just make out Paul sitting by the bed doubled up. I thought it must be a toothache, a liver attack. But no. He was being haunted. He admitted it, and then added, 'It's nothing.' For a long time I thought I had a special task. I had to help Paul, I had to try to understand him. Yet in return, he made me feel that Pauline and I were simply obstacles in his way. And so I changed tack. I bought the most beautiful flowers in the market at Gif. I was such a good customer that they used to give me flowers on top of what I'd bought. I wore pretty white dresses which I starched carefully. I made my hair soft and fluffy. I washed Pauline non-stop, which wasn't always easy. I did everything so that the two obstacles should at least be fresh, bright, perfumed and blossoming. In Paul's eyes I was doing this just in order to make the obstacles greater, to complicate his life yet further.

The period of being obstacles lasted about a year. Every day was very long. Time was suspended. The curtain on the next act went up early one morning. Paul came home having spent the night in the company of the one who haunts him. He was out of his mind, delirious. He spoke to me as if I were not

41

myself but someone else. I felt guilty for not being this other person. The next day he regained his equilibrium and I packed his bag. Pauline and I ceased to exist as obstacles, and straightaway we had more air to breathe, more space in the house. I thought it would be easier to live with someone who was truly absent.

But no, the one who was absent didn't absent himself. Paul no longer spent the nights at Gif, but he came back every day, like a sleepwalker. He would sit down on the kitchen floor and mend Pauline's old toys. He would bring a whole collection of new light bulbs to replace just one that he had noticed was burnt out. Soon after he came with some very beautiful candelabra and yards of electric wires. It's hard to say which I felt more strongly—exasperation at seeing him drifting about in this way, or pity, an affectionate pity, because he was behaving as though, as a result of his departure, Pauline and I were bound to be plunged into darkness.

His attentions upset me. I decided that I

had to be finished with him. For the first time in my life, my health preoccupied me. I had to go on living at whatever cost, for Pauline's sake. I needed a certain freedom to recover my balance, to make a clean sweep. I wanted to banish words like Feeling, Passion, and the like, from my vocabulary. Paul was stopping me from doing so. He found a kind of solace in feeling guilty. He was bent on proving to me that the years we had spent together had created bonds which survived catastrophes. On each of his visits, he referred to these bonds. There is no one who drives in nails more persistently than Paul when he puts his mind to it. In the middle of January he started to embellish his 'bonds' with roses and white lilac. His bonds were becoming too much for me. The motto of Paul Morand's character, the man-who-was-always-in-a-hurry, came to my mind: his motto was 'Quickly and Badly'. Did Paul want to live out all his tragedies that quickly during one lifetime?

'It doesn't seem to be going well for you Paul,' I ventured to say while arranging some

43

flowers in a vase. 'Why should things go well?' he replied in a simple voice as if the search for happiness was a fool's game. Yet fool's game or not, I could read Paul almost like a book. He was in a mess, that is all there was to it. He got up to straighten an icon that was hanging a little crookedly on the wall, and then went and stared through the window at the walnut tree in the neighbour's garden: a tree that he had always liked. Without turning towards me and in the same simple voice, he said: 'To come and live with me, you didn't have to leave anyone.'

That was true. There I had been lucky. My only worry then was about earning enough roubles to buy the winter coat and shoes, so that I could go to the university in a temperature of twenty degrees below zero. I used to call those pennies I earned on the building site my penance. I would say to Paul: 'I earned extra penance today' or: 'No work, no penance.' It was a slip, pure and simple. I had the two words confused. Before learning the word pennies, I knew the word penance,

44

having read it several times in texts on moral philosophy.

Monad—another philosophical term—was more familiar to me than 'promenade' and I would say, 'Let's take a little monad.' I'm sure a lot of people who learn a foreign language make mistakes like this at the beginning. Paul used to make fun of these slips of mine. On the first of January he wrote to me from Paris: 'For others the year is beginning now. For me it began in the summer, during the days of penance.' Paul can give anything a halo of spirituality. Since he stopped living at Gif, he never fails when he comes into the house to take off his shoes, as if he were crossing the threshold of a mosque.

I turn the shoes over. The soles have holes. He has a special way of walking, a little like Chaplin in *City Lights*. Fashionable shoes aren't meant for that. He has holes in his shoes barely a few hours after buying them, and always in exactly the same place. And then he goes on wearing them even in rain or snow. Those holes used to hurt me. As soon as I had earned some royalties, I bought Paul two spare pairs of shoes. That way he would have dry feet for at least a few hours. Now there are other holes which have hurt me. When Paul leaves the house, that makes a hole.

No sooner does he arrive than he has to leave. It's invariable. His arrival signals his departure. I've worked out a whole system of warnings and counter-warnings for myself. But it does no good: the imminence of each of his departures pushes me to a cliff edge. I look down into space and I suffer a kind of vertigo. It soon passes with a hot water bottle or a vinegar compress on the heart, but I am always obliged to lie down. When the moment for departure arrives—and it may be at any time—it is like an event ordained by fate: obediently he puts on his shoes and does his best to leave the house without being noticed. Sometimes I only know he is leaving because I hear Pauline, from downstairs where she is watching the television, shout out: 'See you later, Dad!'

My friend Nastia, who works on hormone

research, tends toward a hormonal explanation of Paul's behaviour. When it was a question of saying, 'I have to leave you and I will,' Paul found a far less direct, a more subtle way of saying it. Indeed it was only his slightly hoarse voice which lent any drama to his words at all. Yet, in reality, Pauline and I could never have been more dramatically left, more thoroughly abandoned, than we were in our state of polite doubt. The politeness meant that Paul had no bad conscience about not being there; his absences did not trouble him. It also meant that Pauline and I were placed in a state of constant confusion concerning his presence and absence. For him to feel good, we had to go out of our minds. Was he perhaps asking too much of us? One evening, while he was taking the air by the open window, I picked up a large vase of flowers and threw it at his head. Undoubtedly my strain of gypsy blood was in revolt and had sought some aid from the dinosaurs and lobsters.

Violence distresses Paul. He can't stand it. 'Now you are going too far.' He admonished me in a courteous but strained voice, while wiping his face and looking out of the corner of his eye to check whether the vase I had broken was his favourite, the white porcelain one with tiny blue flowers. I've rarely known anyone so unpossessive about property as Paul, but when he's thinking, he likes to let his eyes fall on a small number of familiar and simple objects. The white porcelain vase with blue flowers, if not Pauline and I, figured among these objects.

So as not to be throwing vases at him every day, I called on the fundamental patience of the Russian people as embodied in their popular proverbs. That time a more violent proverb came into my mind. 'When the head of somebody is cut off, you no longer mourn his hair.' I could fling all the vases in the world at Paul, I could apply every Russian proverb to his behaviour, he would still continue as before, along the path he had chosen. This inexorability was something I was going to have to admit.

I don't know why I was always washing

myself, I bathed, I showered, I sprinkled. Was I trying to lather myself away? A kind of dissolution? Despite her protests, I washed Pauline too.

I drank water. I ate nothing. 'You've fallen in love,' Nastia said when she saw my jeans flapping around me like a cobbler's apron. 'I'm going to give you some antasthene shots.' Pharmaceutics to redeem ashes! No, it was better to laugh. For a moment, while cleaning the ears of Nastia's baby son with cotton wool on a match stick, I toyed with this unknown colourless word, 'antasthene'.

Nastia's son was called Vassia, after my father who had died that year. It had been a good idea of hers to have a baby somewhat late in life. A new face, new hair, a new voice, mischief, there's nothing like these for giving you a new sense of life. Now Vassia can walk, and tells me his own news over the telephone.

Nastia and Vassia slept at Gif on New Year's Eve. Paul was absent, holding the hand of the one who haunted him. Pauline was away in the mountains. Nastia was happy as a

49

lark. On New Year's morning, it was sunny. The house at Gif has a talent for catching the light. The sun was playing on the walls, the ceilings, the floor. We drank our coffee sitting on the carpet and listening to a Brazilian record which Pauline likes. Vassia asked for some hot chocolate. He drank a drop and spilled the rest on the carpet. Nastia's eyes darkened. I didn't move, I just looked at the chocolate sea and thought: it is happiness for me to have Nastia and Vassia here on New Year's Day.

Loss teaches us the order of things, I think. Once I wept just because Pauline broke the window of the front door. Paul's heart must have already been elsewhere, but I didn't know it. Any more than I knew what he meant when, one evening with friends at dinner, he suddenly said: 'Provided they don't take Liola away from us.' I blushed. I could not see what could possibly take me away from Paul, or Paul from me. Even later, when Paul spelt it out, I didn't at first believe what he said. Only my dreams knew better.

I think people separate long before they realize it. You still walk holding hands, but the path isn't the same one. At times Paul used to lose faith in himself and flounder. He didn't talk about it, but I could feel it happening. With my confidence which was enough for two, I tried to restore his confidence. Indirectly. I began to write books for him, as I would have made children for him. Yet in these books I lived in other places, brought to life other people. It seemed to Paul that I was escaping and he smelt betrayal.

In fact in writing a novel there is something of this: you leave, you take something away from somebody. You also kill a part of yourself even if at the same time you bring another part to life. Perhaps I did go a little fast. I felt loss stalking me and by writing I was trying to lure loss away, or at least make a place for it. There had been too many deaths in one fell swoop: Sonia's, Ludmilla's at Nice, my own father's. I felt a casting adrift, a fear. By telling stories, I tried to exorcize it.

At this time one of Pauline's phrases used to

come back to me again and again: 'It's not
serious,' she would say. This was perhaps the
second thing she ever said after 'Someone
black'. Pauline broke clocks, telephones,
loudspeakers, everything, and then she announced: 'It's not serious.' She knew how to
give herself confidence. 'See you later,' she
said when I left for Moscow. And now that her
father no longer lives here, she says the same
thing each time he goes through the door: 'See
you later.' Pauline asks for no explanation and
looks for no revenge. Her father loves another
woman—it happens so often. She herself goes
on loving him as before, without exuberance
and apparently without any surprise at
whether she sees him or not.

The religion of sexual desire, of 'sexual
satisfaction'—a catch phrase of the time—
makes me ponder. What is more ephemeral
and capricious than Desire? It disturbed me to
see Paul—when everything was still normal—
fall for the magnetism of this new-found God,
this God who prevented him from examining
the stream of images filling his own mind.

52

At that moment Desire brought no images to my mind. But I saw it do so in others. Never before had I noticed men desiring me so insolently in the street. I realized that I could recognize their look, despite my short-sightedness, without even putting on my glasses. I also recognized the meaning of the smile on the lips of unaccompanied women, and the expression of the couples with their arms around one another in the park. For the first time in my life the spectacle of the world was clear to me, eloquent. It was as though a lucidity had replaced my short-sightedness. And this change worried me. I had often told myself that madness was nothing but an extreme lucidity, a lucidity without protection. Soon, thank God, my short-sightedness, both external and internal, returned.

If I look at the polaroid photos which Pauline took of me in those days, I find myself—why not use the word—radiant. Yet how furious I was when Paul, on one of his visits to the house, said to Pauline, who was proudly showing him these photos:

53

'But of course. Your mother is marvellous.'

It was then that I understood how women waste their time, at such critical moments, examining themselves in the mirror or asking whether it has happened because of their wrinkles, or their grey hair, or because their noses or breasts aren't perfectly shaped. Yet how to stop? You look for causes, for mistakes, for a way to do better. What else can you invent at such moments?

I keep mixing up periods in a happy-go-lucky way. Though that's hardly the phrase. The reader must have guessed that I'm not writing these pages for the beauty of the thing, but for other reasons. Or unreasons. Which?

Let's go on. I was trying to discover how to live with absence. With the presence of an absence, with the constant reminder in flesh and blood of an absence. Paul's constant comings and goings were creating havoc. Each time, I had to go round the whole circle again. He, in his triumphant innocence, could never have understood this. It would have been so much easier for me if I could have known that he was far away, on the other side of the ocean, or, if such a luxury was possible, at least in another city. I didn't dare go away myself because of Pauline. She liked the house, her school, her friends, our special neighbours, the garden.

There are people adept at forgetting. And Paul is one of them I think. An instinctive amnesia. Sometimes his lack of memory gets him into trouble. So one can hardly blame him if, at other times, he uses it to protect himself. Without the aid of this amnesia, how would he have been able to come and go, so easily, between his two homes? He did not want to hurt anyone. He thinks everyone is as forgetful as himself.

When I say 'he thinks', it's not quite right. Paul doesn't think. He acts. He moves. He circles in orbit around whatever attracts him, and the attraction illuminates him. The orbits may change but the illumination doesn't. He does everything passionately. At one moment he is attracted to Childhood, at another to the Immediate. At one moment he relearnt Latin to decipher the text of Joan of Arc's two trials; at another he disappeared under photocopies of Blaise Pascal's manuscripts, cut into strips. These strips covered the floors in the house because Paul was looking for an order to them and he needed a panoramic perspective.

After Joan of Arc, I was winded; in face of Pascal, something in me snapped. I went to Madrid with Fenosa. He was having an exhibition there. Among other sculptures there was one of a man carrying a horse on his back. I came back sooner than expected. The telephone rang. It was the first time I heard the voice of the one Paul dreamt about: 'Is Paul there?' I answered that he wasn't. I wasn't lying. Paul was no longer in the house, even if he was. There was a ghost who was called Paul by habit and there were two obstacles, Pauline and Liola. All these characters were approaching the day of judgement. The voice of the one he dreamt about testified to this.

I watch Mother sleeping. Of all this story, she is ignorant. That at least is a comforting thought. I smile. I surprise myself by smiling. I feel a tenderness take over and I am peaceful. It happens that these inexplicable states of peace come upon me. Unexpectedly. Sometimes they last quite a long while. Then I thank the unknown for the unknown, as if the sun's rays or the freshly-opened leaves were personally addressed to me. I shouldn't allow Paul so much importance, so that he even invades this hospital room where Mother is asleep. My forces are gathering strength and closing their ranks. Forward without Paul! When all is said and done, we loved each other so much, he and I, that I have something left to survive on. And now it is Mother, who has no strength left for anything, who is helping me.

She was already unwell last Christmas. She complained of her heart. The Russians wear this organ out. I didn't like the haste with which she wanted to hand over to me all the family photos and the bundle of letters from Paul. I wanted the home, where Mother and Father were living when I first left for France, to last a long time yet. I wanted to bring Pauline there again. And it lasted, this home, for only a few months more.

Amongst the family photos there's one of Mother at my age. Her face is smooth, her hair neatly tied back by a scarf. She's wearing a pre-war dress, Deanna Durbin style—an actress who was popular in Russia then and now forgotten. Her Vassia was to come back from the front with one arm missing, with his back reduced to a pulp by shrapnel, and with head wounds. Sitting on his lap, I came to know his smell. It was mixture of cognac and *eau de cologne* from a bottle with a label on which there was the name of a Greek island which I can't remember. Before the war Father only drank on holidays. This was exceptional among a people who were already living under 'The Chief of Chiefs'. In another photo Father looks very smart in his new lieutenant-colonel's uniform. Stalin changed the cut of all military clothes, so that they looked again like Tsarist uniforms. In place of his arm, amputated at the shoulder, there is an artificial one. The very latest: perfect articulation, pure pigskin, creaking a bit. Father didn't usually wear it. When Pauline and I brought him a beautiful London-made three piece suit from Paris, he put on his artificial arm so that the sleeve would fall better. He forgot his arm one morning and Pauline, nodding towards a glass with Mother's denture in it, whispered, 'Grandma's teeth are there, but where has Grandpa's arm gone?'

Father's hair was white now. Despite his stroke, he still drank. As soon as he knew Pauline and I were coming, he went out with a string bag to buy things. For Pauline, a bear beating a drum and a frog that jumped. For me, caviar and Georgian white wine. For him, I had a bottle of whiskey and a pair of furry doe-skin boots. These boots he immediately christened, 'Bye Bye Youth'.

Tentatively I suggested that he should drink the whisky slowly. A wasted effort. I didn't want to annoy him too much. He never annoyed me. He got drunk mellowly. He talked about the war, about me as a little girl. Much to Pauline's surprise, he sang a duet with Mother. Pauline had never heard or seen a duet. In the song they sang, there was a couplet about the 'blue scarf that you wore on your darling shoulders' and another about a soldier at the front staring at the fire in the stove and thinking: 'It's not easy to reach you, and Death is a few steps away.'

Father always said he was incredibly lucky to be wounded. It was on the day of his thirty-third birthday. His friends had arranged a party for him in a dug-out. The alcohol was 90% proof. This was all there was to drink on the Leningrad front and the only way of keeping warm. Before the party began, Father was rehearsing the plans for a 'defensive attack' in the General Staff dug-out a few yards away. He and his fellow officers received the signal that everything was ready for the party. They ran across the few yards which were exposed to enemy fire. A bomb exploded. All of them were killed except Father.

'We both escaped,' Father once told me

when he had drunk some vodka. 'Death passed under our very noses and we are both alive!' He was referring to an illness I suffered a few months after the war started. About this illness I remember only what Father and Mother told me later. Icicles, it appears, were its cause. I would not stop eating icicles during the March of '41. They were everywhere, on the shutters of the house, along the pavillion in the square where Mother took me for walks. As soon as her back was turned, I started crunching them. One night I collapsed with a very high temperature and a throat so swollen I could scarcely breathe. Father was completing his studies in military strategy at the Lenin Academy in Moscow and we were living in the suburbs. My symptoms started to be alarming: blue spots appeared all over my body. There weren't many trains at night, so Father wrapped me in an eiderdown, picked me up in his arms and started running along the road with the idea of stopping the first car that came by. There weren't many cars either, and of the few that passed, none stopped. We were not in luck. The drivers who weren't stopping, had survived the purges, had the means to run a car, and they were driving at night towards Moscow from a suburb famous for its wealthy dashas—such people were bound to be shits. The minutes passed. I was turning bluer and bluer and breathing less and less. What could he do? Father had the right to be armed on account of his military studies, and so, clasping me in the eiderdown under one arm, he pulled out his revolver with the other and fired into the air. A car stopped. A few minutes later I was in the Botkin Hospital with a probe down my throat.

Any night without sleep is long. The new blood bottle is already half empty. Mother is very still, too still. Too much of her strength has left her. Too much? What am I trying to measure? Is 'too much' a reasonable quantity? Can one be abandoned 'too much'? Don't such things imply that the limit has already been reached?

One night last summer in Patmos there was a strong wind blowing. There were five of us, two men and three women waiting for a car. The two men, with their backs to the wind, put their arms around their women to protect them. I wasn't protected, but it was not important for I had a shawl which Paul had given me when I was expecting Pauline, a blue traditional Orenburg shawl. These shawls are still made in Russia despite state planning. We were happy, Pauline and I, on that island. I spent my mornings with Jeanne, typing in front of a window which looked out onto a pile of gravel where a terrace was being rebuilt. Pauline and my friend, Franca, went off to do sea-diving and to fish for sea urchins. I stayed alone, happy to be able to get on with my book and watch a family of cats. The mother cat had chosen the pile of gravel as a shelter for her young. One day she disappeared, taking her family with her. But she forgot one kitten. He was completely wild. I've never seen his like. Nevertheless, he had to eat. On a stone near his hole, I put a saucer of milk. In my absence he drank it. Each new saucer I then left made him braver. Eventually he became so bold that he came up to my window and stared in at me, but only when it was shut, never when it was open. He devoured the remains of his first New Zealand chicken—which I gave him—like a tiger.

Why were all provisions on Patmos imported from New Zealand? 'Strange correspondences exist,' said Pauline gravely, with a look of the Close Encounter kind, 'between islands.' Pauline adores both celestial and earthly maps. She can't be without an atlas any more than Paul can be without newspapers. Paul gets up like a shot in the morning, drinks his coffee and reads the morning papers in a café. This is why he can't take holidays. There was no question of his coming to the island. I took a firm grip of myself and started to breathe the Grecian air with which so much began; for instance, I never tired of hearing the word *apocalipsis*. We heard it constantly as we approached the sea in our bus full of women dressed in black, who crossed themselves at ever corner. At first I thought they were afraid of being flung into the ditch, but they were simply crossing themselves each time we passed a chapel.

It was on the isle of Patmos that Saint John received his revelations, in a cave not far from where we were staying.

'How did this man,' Pauline asked me, 'who you said was Jesus' favourite disciple, land up here? Patmos is a long way from Israel.'

I answered vaguely: 'Yes, a long way. It suited the Romans, who were lousy colonialists, to send him to Patmos, as far away as possible, to get rid of him.'

'Oh, I see,' said Pauline. 'Patmos is like Magadan.'

It did something to me to hear Pauline use that word. 'Yes Pauline, if you like it's a little like Magadan, but Magadan is even further away from Moscow than Patmos is from the Promised Land. The sky there isn't so blue or so clear. The earth stays frozen, even in summer. Frozen earth, frozen fog, glacial winds, grey sea, terrifying rocks. Everything has been arranged so that a man there feels he is at the end of the world, surrounded by enemies, forgotten by God. And he is both hungry and thirsty. A man? Countless men, as numerous as ants in an anthill. Saint John, you know, was lucky to be alone, surrounded by vineyards and fig trees. He could sit in his cool cave with his secretary and dictate his visions. He was free to eat or to fast. He could walk in the valley where the sheep graze. He was free to contemplate the sky or talk to his God. He was free.'

'Free—what does that mean, Liola?'

Pauline uses my first name whenever she wants to show that she feels independent. I stopped talking. A long silence. Pauline waited, meditated on my lack of an answer, came up close to me, kissed me and went away.

I look at the gravel. There is no kitten. The typewriter is silent. There it is. I'm at Magadan. I have lived within my imagination so many long hours at Magadan, spent so much time with the prisoners, they have so filled my heart and mind, that now I can see with my own eyes how dawn breaks at Magadan: the black file of prisoners winding through the snow, the guards armed with rifles, the dogs. They come to Magadan from every corner of my country. The first circles are already behind them. Once arrived there, they have lost everything: everything, that is, that normally sustains you: family, children, loved ones. All that they have are their bodies—more or less alive—and their minds. The more one loses, the less one has to lose. And so, perhaps, the less one is afraid. The more one may be free. Prisons exist not only where there is the maximum of barbed wire and the most dogs. That madness which makes people imprison *themselves* may be cured by the Magadan snow. This is the terrifying paradox that Kostia expounded to me one afternoon in his little hotel bedroom facing Montparnasse cemetery.

Kostia met his mother at Magadan after fifteen years of separation. She had been freed, but she did not have the right to leave. She was in Magadan in forced residence. 'In

Moscow,' Kostia said, 'they were dying of fear. I had just come from there and I'd seen it. But here in Magadan, they talked calmly of everything, just as you and I might talk in Paris.'

Kostia described Magadan to me in geographical detail. I could feel that his words were now ready to go to the printers. But they were so compelling, so alive, that they made me think of Fenosa under his palm tree in the morning, modelling clay as naturally as he breathed.

At the time of the 'Moscow Spring' during a few months at the end of the fifties and the beginning of the sixties, Kostia was spoken of as 'the Russian Hemingway'. When I first met him, he was already beginning to change. A story of his, which I had just read, was nothing like Hemingway. It was a very short story which told of a chess game between chance partners on a train, but already Magadan was in it. I could feel it. They were pages written with the sensibility of a Proust by a man who had faced the Stalinist terror. For me when I first met him, Kostia was the author of those pages. He was sitting on the floor in a Moscow flat. On the table stood a bottle of English gin, a slab of black bread, and a tall tin in which dried fish were standing upright. These tins of fish are especially designed for eating in submarines. To find them in Moscow is as strange as it would be to find Volga caviar in Patmos. The flat belonged to Andrei and we were sitting in the kitchen. Andrei's wife was away on holiday and there wasn't much food. How distant that evening now seems, especially so because two of my friends who were there are no longer alive. Ludmila and Sonia are dead. Kostia sat on the floor and drank gin and said little. Mother and Father were looking after Pauline in the Kuntsevo flat. I, too, was drinking gin. Sonia wasn't coughing yet. Kostia was making her laugh. Nothing much happened, nothing much was said. It is like a landscape in a mist. Yet it was only seven years ago.

The man talking to me about Magadan in the hotel bedroom with the empty Schweppes

bottles, overlooking the cemetery of Monta-
parnasse is the same Kostia. He is sitting on his
bed. I'm sitting next to him in an armchair.
The day before yesterday I packed Paul's bag.
Yesterday I told Pauline that Paul was no
longer going to sleep in the house. Today I
have come back to life. It is many years since
I've looked at a man, except Paul, as I look at
Kostia now. Of the Kostia I knew in Moscow,
I recognize only the eyes, their blue, their
smile and their sadness. It's as if he has grown
smaller, both his face and body. Yet he has a
new moustache and a new haircut. His hair is
longer and slightly wavy. The room seems
very hot to me. We laugh, though there isn't
so much to laugh about. To hell with time and
difference! My Magadan brother and I have
well and truly met again and we are drinking
Schweppes in front of the Montparnasse
cemetery.

It's not a cemetery I like, but then I don't
like the cemeteries here. In Russia the earth
rests lightly on the bodies of the dead, or so one
imagines. Here all these vast blocks of stone

70

are too heavy. They are monuments to a civilized, cultured death, to investment death. Nevertheless, the cemetery of Montparnasse isn't just a collection of stones for me. One day, as we walked along the path which leads to the windmill, Paul told me that his first child, a boy, was buried there. And Renée is there. Renée, to whom I owe a great deal, Renée, who in the early days guided me through the labyrinth of French conjugations, agreements and articles. Unfortunately neither my clowning throughout our Russian translation sessions, nor my vegetable soups, were able to help her in return. Renée had the temerity to stake everything on one man and she fell from a height of six storeys.

For Kostia Montparnasse is a virgin cemetery. Yet Magadan speaks to us both far more loudly than our different pasts. We have our losses in common, as well as our achievements. We Russians have all come out of Magadan. We sit there quietly sipping a non-alcoholic drink, sharing an agreement we could never define. Some time after that evening in

71

Andrei's flat Kostia gave up drinking. From that evening, he tells me, he remembers only one thing: the image of a young woman with chestnut eyes, wearing a simple well-cut dress, who laughed and kept her distance. I listen to him talking about this woman with interest, for a few months ago I left her skin. She was another Liola whom one day I will perhaps have to find again. As he goes on talking, I discover that Kostia lost himself too; before I did, at about the time of the dried fish for submarines, when he gave up drinking. When a Russian stops drinking, it's like becoming an outlaw. First he goes into hiding, then into exile. Kostia and I compare our exiles.

Sometimes this famous war which men and women wage against one another, makes me smile. The differences are so small compared to what we have in common. And from just a few differences, a kind of racism develops; everything then becomes the fault of the other race.

When I first met Paul, he had already lived, while I wasn't much, I was more like a project.

I felt very strongly what life might be like and I was an ideal spectator. Paul appeared to me to be not only a man, but a world. He belonged to the category of miracles. You aren't surprised by a miracle. You feel possessed and calmed by it. So this can happen! So it's normal. Paul was my marvellously normal man. Marvellous like his letters. These may have complicated the life of the KGB censors working in the Moscow Post Office, but to me they were a world, a whole new perspective, a spectacle I couldn't grow tired of. Yet, to a certain point I was to remain a spectator, as if things weren't really happening to me.

My short-sightedness may have something to do with it. People who see well don't think about seeing. So they can see less. For the short-sighted, for the really myopic, seeing itself is an act. And so they see more. The world is perhaps further away in terms of sight, but it is more present. My eyes have also helped me survive. My eyes, in my hardest moments, permitted me to relegate Paul's

73

shoes or his anxious face during his fleeting visits, to a vague half-distance where, thankfully, they were reduced to a simple spectacle.

Liola, sitting next to her Magadan brother, closes her eyes and becomes a woman again. She is no longer preventing someone else from living, but allowing herself to live. In front of the lift, just before we say goodbye, Kostia touches my lips with his. The blood rises to my cheeks, my heart pounds. It hasn't beaten like that for years, except out of sorrow.

Next Christmas, Kostia was in Moscow and I was visiting there. He brought me in his car to see Mother. Mother didn't say a word to him, she simply watched him out of the corner of her eye, a look I knew so well. In fact he was the type of man she would normally have liked, well-dressed, celebrated, a writer. She simply held it against him that he wasn't Paul. That was all. Mother was always the same. She would never ask me how Paul treated me, but how I treated Paul. Father, on the other hand, ended his letters with the question: 'Is Paul still kind to you?'

All of my more unconventional, adventurous acts won my father's support. When I told him about what happened in the 'short trials' which took place in that bastion of Marxist ideology, the Philosophy Faculty, trials officially termed Komsomol Meetings, he listened with great interest. It was Mother who interrupted: 'Not so fast, my little pigeon. Don't stir things up. There is only one thing you have to do and that's keep quiet. You can't defend everyone. One day you'll have to pay for that kind of thing.'

During that first year at university, I took up the defence of a boy called Levy. His only sin was that he invented stories. A mythomaniac. He invented a great love: his wife. He invented a little son: David, aged three. These were his only topic of conversation. He always kept us up to date on his wife's medical check-ups, his son's vaccinations. 'David is in hospital. I'll be able to give you more news of him tomorrow, I'm going to see him tonight.' And we would rush out and buy oranges or a story book with illustrations.

Then a Komsomol meeting was announced. The agenda for the day read: 'First, Budapest. Second, The Moral Character of Alexander Levy.'

After Alberto, an Italian communist student of rare intelligence, whom I liked a lot, had shed his light on events in Budapest, the examination of Alexander Levy's moral character was announced. I couldn't sit still. We were about to be 'illuminated' as they used to say.

We were told that the said Alexander Levy had neither wife nor child, that he made use of this imaginary family to skip classes and to sit exams at odd times, in short that he was a corrupt degenerate. The adjective 'capitalist' wasn't used, but it came to the same thing. Alexander Levy stood by the side of the praesidium rostrum. I looked at his red hair, his thin body, his worn grey suit. In the satchel for my books, I had two oranges for his son David: the son who was in hospital; the son who, according to the comrades, didn't exist in reality. One after another the students went

up to the rostrum and so abused Alexander
Levy that the fact that he had neither wife nor
son no longer shocked or surprised me. To
invent a wife and a son seemed to me as
plausible a way as any other for getting
through a life. What did shock me was the
students' hatred, the cheapness of their argu-
ments, the filth that they were heaping on
Alexander Levy. They were using lies which
far surpassed his: and whereas his lie touched
me, theirs were disgusting. To destroy the last
shreds of Alexander Levy's moral character,
the final orator brandished before the dumbfounded public a medical certificate which
testified that Levy had gonorrhea. I was
furious. Two friends tried to hold me back.
They clutched at my skirt. But they couldn't
stop me. I arrived at the rostrum, and I made
a fateful speech which ensured that during the
next five years, I would always risk being
accused of every possible subversion. My
errors were categorized as those of an 'abstract
humanist'.

Only later was I to learn how qualified in

humanism my colleagues were. Krushchev, with all his reformative zeal, had decided to change the security services from top to bottom. He did so, but this meant recycling countless people who lost their jobs. The denunciations, the tortures, the assassinations —there had been so many accomplices, so many jobs! Among these freshly unemployed, some of the young ones, those of thirty or thirty-five, had been judged recuperable by the mother ideology, and a number of them had ended up in the Philosophy Faculty of Moscow University: that same Faculty to which my own thirst for knowledge had drawn me.

On my arrival in this ideological nursery, I was amazed to see so many strange worn-out men, who seemed to me as old as the world. I had no idea who they were. I can still see myself, as if it were only yesterday, at the first Russian Composition exam. On either side, my fellow examinees lent towards me, whispering questions. They knew nothing about grammar or spelling or vocabulary. It was incredible. It was inconceivable that they had come out of secondary schools. So where had they come from?

There were two girls of my own age. I was eighteen. We sat together, surrounded by sixty students of the opposite sex who were twice our age. From the start I took a dislike to these men. I should add that they were dowdy, with grey skin, bags under their eyes, thin hair and unpleasant breath.

Maybe it had not been so easy on the other side of the barricades! When I think of the slenderness, the beauty of Kostia's mother after seventeen years in the Gulag, of the vitality and freshness of my friend Andrei, who, after twenty-seven years spent behind the Urals as an Enemy of the People, now lives in the Bois de Boulogne with his dog and cats, I sense a new and monstrous paradox growing. The enemies of the people, when they are not murdered, fare better than their executioners.

Our policeman-philosophers were certainly in a bad state, but this did not prevent them blustering. Coarsely and lewdly. Afflicted with various ailments—of the liver, stomach, heart, bladder—they ate in the Special Diets Section of the University Cafeteria. Nevertheless, they still had all kinds of short and long-term sexual plans concerning those of us who didn't eat in that cafeteria. Because I refused their propositions, I was undoubtedly granted the honour of being added to their list of Potential Enemies of the People.

I was to pay the price of this later after the rudiments of my Belgian French had led to my encounter with Paul. Paul would come to meet me in the University Hall on Moknovaia Street, just opposite the Kremlin. He used to stroll along the corridor leading to the library. He even used the toilets. This was perfectly understandable since outside it was snowing and freezing. But for our new philosophers and one-time night-watchman of ideology, everything Paul did was suspect. He was prying into the most secret places of the body of socialist construction. He wasn't a member of the French Communist Party,

80

he didn't write for the Communist press. And so he was a spy, disguised as a bourgeois journalist.

And now it was to be my turn for a trial and a warning. Clearly the new philosophers, while leafing through their Hegel or Kant, had remained in touch with the 'special branch' of Lomonossov University, who still had close links with their former organization. And their vengeance bore fruit.

My physical appearance began to alarm Mother. I lost pounds. I was pale. Paul kept leaving and coming back. And if one day he didn't come back? No, Mother protested against herself, that she couldn't believe! Paul was Paul and her little Liola wasn't a young woman to be left in the lurch! I told her nothing of the interrogations which were monthly, then weekly and finally daily. My friends among both students and professors, who knew what was going on behind my back, kept telling me: 'Forget your Frenchman. Here you have a future in front of you, at least a scientific future! As for the rest. . . , you'll

81

manage like we do.' I was determined not to give in. Each morning I got myself an injection and with its help I could endure the cross-examinations, I could argue back, I could even get angry enough to slam the door in their faces.

I was twenty when I loved Paul. Perhaps it was this more than the morning injections which gave me my strength. Fifteen years later when I was again summoning up all my strength, this time to throw Paul out, I was only helping him to realize one of his dreams. Just as, earlier, I had recognized and defended Alexander Levy's right to have a dream: his right to invent a child and a great love for himself, because this made it easier for him to live. Alexander Levy had killed and harmed nobody, and the disappointment I felt at not being able to give two oranges to his son, David, was nothing compared to what he must have suffered before inventing his dream. He was Jewish; I wasn't. He already knew a thousand things about what was going on which I would only learn later. He was more desperate than I, and he had reason to be. And probably he was more honest than I. I hadn't reasoned things out during the Komsomol meeting. None of my actions was very conscious, I was simply carried along by a force which came to me from afar, perhaps the same force which, one day in October fifteen years later, enabled me to pack Paul's bag. Paul, who had a wife and child who weren't imaginary.

It was a very warm autumn. By the window at Gif both the apples from the trees and the night, seemed to be falling together. Plouf! We listened together, Kostia and I, Kostia who was leaving for Moscow the next day. Is there anything better on this earth than recognizing one another in the night, when we are at last ourselves?

The French say: 'Vivre sa vie'. To live one's life. Jean-Luc used the phrase as a title for a film. He knows that it is untrue. We don't live our lives. We are lived by life.

Another Swiss filmmaker, Michel—whom Paul likes and I do too because he is honest and generous—was waiting in his car for his wife Andrienne. Andrienne I think was at the dentist's. Michel is reading the script for a television film he's making. He raises his head and notices Jean-Luc who is standing by a bus stop in the middle of the road; clearly he must be waiting to go to Geneva, whilst Michel is going to Lausanne. So Michel does nothing. He holds Jean-Luc in such esteem that he doesn't want to take him by surprise by tooting and perhaps interrupting a stream of thought. It's a pity, thinks Michel, for he can very well see that Jean-Luc, standing in the sun, is much too hot. It's scarcely the beginning of spring, more like the end of winter, but the heat is oppressive. That morning, Jean-Luc had put on a heavy beige woollen suit—one of those ill-fitting suits he likes so much; he didn't know it was going to be so hot. Michel goes back to reading his script. Five minutes later, he looks up again. Jean-Luc has disappeared. He's taken the bus, Michel thinks, and Andrienne hasn't come yet. He goes on reading for another ten

84

minutes. He looks up again, Jean-Luc is there, standing in exactly the same spot. Only now, he is holding a white bulging plastic bag, and he's wearing a suit of a nondescript grey, made of a nondescript synthetic fabric, even less smart than the previous one, but much lighter. It is a suit absolutely without character, such as only Jean-Luc knows how to find. He must have found it in the supermarket opposite. He doesn't move, he is waiting. He is feeling better, less hot. Then through his sun glasses he notices Michel in his car. Michel, a little shy and fascinated by the change of clothes, the lack of fuss, the insousiance of the whole scene, waves to Jean-Luc. Jean-Luc, who now guesses that Michel has followed the whole sequence of events, gives Michel a faint, brief smile, a minimal smile. Then he jumps into the bus which has just drawn up.

This story, which Michel told to Paul and Paul to me, made an impression on me. Partly because I know Jean-Luc's minimal smile and partly because, imagining this scene, I see

Jean-Luc living his life, or rather being obedient to it. A simple change of temperature obliges a stubborn man like Jean-Luc to go through a whole series of actions. He may go through them hurriedly, with his eyes shut, and of course without a thought about how he may appear to others. Nevertheless, the change of temperature obliges him to go through these actions. Life lived Jean-Luc. And Jean-Luc, because he has grace, slipped past his partner, life. Such grace is very rare, a tiny breath of air between two doors, between two words, a tiny light which is almost nothing, and yet a gift. Sometimes, Jean-Luc emits this light, briefly, intimately, like one of his grave, vague smiles.

He and Paul shared something. They could sit opposite one another for hours on end without saying a word. In front of Jean-Luc, Paul felt like a nobody. He didn't tell me this and he didn't suffer from it. Paul has always been too much of a masochist to suffer—on top of everything else—from the failures he invents for himself. They were like two brothers. Now Paul misses Jean-Luc deeply. Yet for ten years, they haven't seen each other. How can I doubt Paul's faculty of forgetfulness?

Mother has turned towards the wall. I can no longer see her hollow cheeks. I see only Xenia turned toward the wall; this was the moment for which Father used to wait so that he could go and take a swig from the bottle of vodka which he had hidden behind the bath.

The Xenia-Vassia couple began with a sack of flour. During the year '28–'29, which our historians no longer refer to as the year of 'Stalin's accession', Mother had already given birth to a son. Her first husband—she used to tell me about him—was odd. He beat her. She had a lot of trouble getting rid of him. Then she found herself alone with her baby in the Ukraine. The Ukraine was also going through a hard time: collectivization and industrialization. At night Mother would barricade her door, because her ex-husband, who had an important job in the local Soviet, was doing everything in his power to try to get her back. At that time Vassia was working in a flour mill and he had taken note of Mother's difficult position. And so, one evening, covered in white flour, a sack over his shoulder, he knocked at her door. The sack meant that Mother and her baby could survive for at least another month.

My Aunt Tanya used to tell me that Father in those days was irresistible, he could seduce anyone he chose even without a sack of flour. He sang. He played the guitar. He didn't drink. When he worked at the mill, he was only nineteen. Mother was twenty-four. They got married straightaway because Father had to leave to do his military service in Kiev.

Today, before coming to the hospital, I spent the day with Aunt Tanya. She is my mother's sister. Tonight she left for the Ukraine, for the house where I was born and where Father delivered his sack of flour. I wanted her to rest and eat before taking the train. I also wanted to see her alone. Soon she

would be the only survivor from my childhood, the last member of my family.

The porter took Aunt Tanya's luggage up
to my room. There was her suitcase with a
strap around it. It seemed to me she had had
this case since the beginning of time. There
were two boxes tied up with cord. There were
string bags in which I could see toilet paper
(this fortnight, thanks to some Plan, there was
shortage throughout the Soviet Union), tins of
Bulgarian food, a salami from the charcuterie
at Gif.

'Now,' I said, 'We're going downstairs.'

'But Liolitchka, I'm not well enough
dressed. Everything's crumpled and anyway,
I'm wearing grey. Let's have something in the
room. No one will see us.'

'You are neither crumpled, nor grey. Come
on.'

I put a pink scarf round her shoulders and
dragged her to the lift. She looked like an
apple, slightly wrinkled, but above all, sun-
drenched. Taking her courage in two hands,
she crossed the hotel lobby full of foreigners.

How these foreigners dress themselves up for their visit to the Homeland of Socialism needs to be seen to be believed! We got to the restaurant. Aunt Tanya had never seen it before, and it was beautiful. A large room under a glass dome, wooden panels, big tables, sculptures, candelabra, white well-starched linen, carpets, fountains, green plants. Two waiters in black jackets rushed forward to welcome us. The room was empty: it was too early, only noon. We were given a big table for two. After a little white wine, my Aunt was completely at her ease. We forgot about Mother, not really, but a little, the weight of the last few days was slightly lifted, we grew younger.

For two months Aunt Tanya had been away from her house in the Ukraine, her house with her two dogs, her cats, her rabbits, her goats, the coal that she puts in the stove each morning. For two months, despite her age, it was she who had been looking after Mother in Moscow. She hadn't wanted me to be told of the gravity of Mother's illness but I came nonetheless. She had been the nurse. Aunt Tanya is like that. She has always assumed and taken responsibility. Her father and mother, my grandparents, both died when she was fourteen. She became the head of the family. Her little sister, my mother, was eight, and her brother, Uncle Vanya, was three. The Imperialist War, as the Russians call the war of 1914; then the Revolution, then the Civil War. It was always a question of finding enough to eat and Aunt Tanya used her wits. With the wood from logs and with old potato sacks, she made shoes which she sold. With this money, she bought tripe and flour and made meat patés which Mother, still a little girl, used to sell in the nearest railway station.

Their house was the one in which I was born. After the war I used to come every year from Moscow to spend the summer there. Its floors smell of freshly washed planks of wood. At night, the sky is very low and black. The windows are open and in the house there is the scent of mint, of roses, of ripe tomatoes. From the house you can hear trains and their

91

whistles. I see myself there, especially from the age of about ten. I washed the floor, I cut up the vegetables for the borscht. At night Uncle Vanya would come home and I would play the fool. There was a neighbour, a young girl, who was dying of tuberculosis. In the evening she came round to our house and I clowned for her. I clowned with all my might, because when she laughed she looked less pale. Besides I knew how real clowns went about it. Thanks to Father I had seen them.

When he came back from the front, Father needed a little amusement. We had left the village in the Urals for the town of Tchkalov, where, despite his wounds, he had to await army orders. Then the Moscow Circus turned up in Tchkalov. I developed a passion for one of the clowns. After the day's work, Father and I would go to the circus. We knew all the acts by heart, and they scarcely interested me any more. It was the life backstage which attracted me. The smell of sawdust and of animals, and my elephant Josef who slept next to the dressing room of our clown. I say 'our' because he was Father's friend as well as mine.

There is still for me something peculiarly dramatic about this backstage life of the circus. There was a man who slashed his wrists for a tightrope walker. There was a dancer who killed herself for love by throwing herself under the feet of her horse. Even the war, in those circus tents, didn't put personal tragedies into perspective. And I, I loved my clown.

'Mother,' I would say, 'I'm going out. I want this scarf, this skirt, this blouse.' Father would take my hand and we would set out on our adventure. Our clown's name was Salomon. Monia for short. He was making up in his dressing room. I watched him. When he began, he was a person like Father; then he was no longer a person at all, but something else. In front of the mirror with the electric light bulbs around it, he dabbed his face with reds, blues, blacks, greens, and while he worked he drank with Father, a mixture of vodka and beer. The two never stopped talking. I no longer remember about what.

Now that Father's dead, I wish I could remember. Not even Aunt Tanya can tell me, for at that time she was in the German-occupied Ukraine.

I spent only my holidays with Aunt Tanya, yet after each visit I noticed a change in myself, a growing-up which was more marked than any I noticed after months at school. What was it that was so special about her? Why did she have this power?

When you were with her, the world began to sing, the simplest things became appealing: gathering grass for the rabbits; feeding the ducks at the bottom of the garden; eating the eggs of these ducks. They were gigantic and they were our principal source of protein. The monstrous size of the eggs repelled me, but my Aunt, through a long ritual she invented, made me forget this. For me she was like a good witch, and she ran a kind of chemist's shop. She never bought the medicines which the sick came to get from her; she made them herself. She made aspirin from a fermented sugar which she extracted from willow trees

94

along the Dnieper on certain prescribed days of the year. She always treated herself with her own medicines and they must have agreed with her. She is straight and upright; her hair has kept its beautiful chestnut colour; her skin, though wrinkled, is very fresh; her eyes are brilliant; her voice is firm, and she is seventy-eight. And now, in one of Moscow's most snobbish restaurants, she was a hundred per cent herself. I like people who manage to be themselves in all circumstances, who are at home with whatever is at hand.

In the Zelenograd flat, before Mother was taken to hospital, I had impressed my Aunt with a fish I cooked. I just threw it with some vegetables and herbs, not in the oven. For her there was something comic about this fish, its taste, the fact that it was so easy to cook. And now, in the restaurant, she wanted to eat fish again. The maître d'hôtel was pouring the Tsinandali into the crystal-stemmed glasses. She must have found the ritual and the luxury a little shocking, yet she smiled, and paid little attention to those who were serving us. They, on the contrary, were fascinated by the odd couple we made. Their usual clientele belonged to a smart set of high-ranking officers, of rich Georgians, of political bosses escorting women in heavy make-up and vulgar, extravagant dresses; if it weren't for the nouveau-riche vulgarity of what they wore, some of these women would be beautiful. It is difficult to be a woman in the Soviet Union, even more difficult than in the West.

The usual clientele of the Metropole eat voraciously, drink enough to die of the next day, and dance to the din of a retro orchestra with a fat singer in lamé who howls into a mike. How far away such a Moscow restaurant is from the way ordinary Russians eat! We usually eat in the kitchen, home-made food. And it's there that we talk for hours, relaxed, affectionate. Even in the days of scarcity and terror, there was always a little warm happiness in our kitchens. There was such happiness in my parents' kitchen in the old Kuntsevo flat, where I did my homework on the corner of the polished table. It was the same at my brother's and my schoolfriends'. It is the same today at the flat of my actor friend in Herzen Street. In my own kitchen at Gif, or in Nastia's at Montrouge, or Nekrassov's in Pigalle, we re-create this happiness. Even on the isle of Patmos, in a Greek shipowner's palace in which we were camping, we established a kind of Russian kitchen, where we drank tea and listened to Victor Platono-vitch talking.

Aunt Tanya smiled. I had the feeling I was living a decisive moment. Mother was leaving me. Paul had already left. With these two losses I had to go on living, and I had nobody, except for a little while longer, my Aunt Tanya, to help me find the old Liola again. The Liola who had been so good at living, so full of unshakeable hope, the Liola who had been both a fighter and a clown. We were eating the fish and I was looking for this Liola who had become as ghostly as the white flour on Father's shoulders when he came to ask Mother to marry him.

The jig-saw puzzle I was trying to put

together was the same one I'd broken into pieces with Paul's complicity. This had happened without either of us being aware of it. I'll never be able to do justice to Paul's innocence. We were, we are, whatever happens, grafted one to another. There is no virtue in this. We both have the same score, a score chalked up by fear. This is why, as I sat there looking at my Aunt, I was perhaps too bruised, too lost.

'A little more?' I poured some Tsinandali into my Aunt's wine glass. We were talking of simple truths. 'You drink wine, you eat fish, you are alive, your blood is being pumped through your body, you are not losing blood. In that case one is lucky, don't you think so Auntie?'

'No!' Aunt Tanya disagreed with my definition of luck. She was looking at me oddly, a little obliquely. It didn't seem right to her that I, who was so young and so successful (this was the word she and Mother used when talking about me), it didn't seem right to her that I should continually define Life by its negative complement which is Death. Death was at Mother's door, not mine. I was going to stay. Aunt Tanya was no longer on my side, and for once she didn't know how to react. She didn't want to follow me; I was frightening her.

One night long ago, in the very same restaurant of the Metropole, I danced with Paul. It wasn't easy. We were trying to match our steps in a way which would go on for years and years. The next day Paul was leaving for Paris. We weren't married yet. While dancing, I was doing my utmost to make my illusions true. Paul has the capacity to switch on people's illusions: he's a lamplighter, like Fenosa's grandfather. He walks on, he wanders around and he forgets to put out his lamps. 'But why are they alight?' he asks. 'I couldn't have done that, I'm not that clever.' At each step he is totally innocent. The more lamps he lights, the more he forgets and becomes modest.

I wiped out this memory of dancing in the same restaurant and said whatever came into

99

my head, so as to dispel the sadness I was beginning to communicate to my Aunt. I talked
without thinking about the tomatoes which
grow crazily on the balcony of my bedroom
at Gif, about the flowers Paul buys for Pauline
and me, about other presents. We sounded a
perfect family. I said nothing about chucking
Paul out.

Regularly and stubbornly I repeated to
Paul, 'If only you would not come back to the
house any more, you wouldn't have to leave.'
It seemed so simple to me. I always tried to
communicate with Paul in simple words. But
they fell into a void.

When Paul stopped sleeping in the house,
I didn't want to see any more the bed which
he had bought before my arrival in France.
With the help of a neighbour, Paul carried
the bed down to the cellar. 'First they kick
the man out of the door; then they throw
out the mattress!' He said this in a
very gentlemanly fashion and we all three
laughed.

In Aunt Tanya's house there were bookshelves. By the age of nine, I knew what happened when a beautiful noblewoman had an assignation at night with her gamekeeper in an arbour on the edge of a precipice! I flipped through the pages of the yellow magazine, *Niva*, which dated from before the Revolution. There, for the first time, I saw engraved in black ink the body of a naked young woman. It was moving, even more so because the scene was a morgue: the reader discovered the body at the same time as the doctor who was just lifting the sheet. Every summer I went back to this engraving which so fascinated me, and every summer my own growing body resembled a little more that of the dead woman's: the same forms, the same lines. She could only just have died, for she seemed so alive lying there on the table. And the doctor's gesture was so pathetic. In the Soviet Union there are no statues in public squares of nude women. On Aunt Tanya's bookshelves there were also poems by Tioutchev, a writer who is not mentioned in our school books. 'I remember those times, those golden

101

times, and everything in me grows hot.' 'In these late days of the year, a moment comes when something gasps in us like the breath of spring.' In Tioutchev's rather bad poems my ten-year-old heart found an assurance, a guarantee of permanence. They didn't make me dream, they gave me strength. I remembered this strength now and wanted to ask my Aunt about her house and the spring and the summer. But we had no time, and we couldn't afford to miss the train. I had to see my Aunt off properly. I fetched her luggage, found a taxi, put the carrier bags on her seat, arranged the suitcases in the luggage rack, and then went to get her some oranges. She couldn't leave for her small town without oranges, which are one of the principal sources of Vitamin C in winter. Whole families were asleep on the benches in the station. There was a lot of marble, and in a large baroque buffet, there were sausages and gherkins, but there were no oranges. I write the word 'oranges' and I'm finished. I can't go on.

Pistol shots can sometimes save your life. We've seen that. Thanks to the pistol shots, my body, ready for the morgue, found its oxygen. In the Botkin hospital I had to stay in a little room for what seemed, to a three-year-old, an eternity. An entire wall of this room, giving on to the hall, was made of glass. The nurses could watch me without having to come in. My illness was thought to be infectious and I was not allowed any visitors. But on my left there was a window, behind which, several times a day, Father appeared. Through the window I watched him perform all the tricks he had learnt from our clown. Once he brought a prop with him, it was an orange. He had nothing else in his pockets. I couldn't hear what he said through the thick glass. With just the orange, he acted out a whole play, and behind him was a backdrop of snow, frozen trees and blue sky. That same morning I had undergone a serious operation without anaesthetic. Two strong male nurses had held my arms and legs while an abscess on my bottom, caused by the injections I had

103

been hurriedly given on arrival, was lanced. I was devastated, not because of the pain the scalpel caused me, but because of the nurses' violence. I had never before experienced violence. The orange Father was playing with made me forget it all.

I return to the beach in Catalonia. I am swimming and then I come out of the sea and I notice one of Franco's policemen in uniform, dragging a dog along with a hideous instrument. It's a stick, long, thick, rigid. At the end there's a large chain. The instrument permits the dog to be caught and then be held at a distance while he's dragged towards the pound vehicle. The dog undergoes torture. He can't breathe. He is struggling and can barely yelp. His eyes look mad. Shocked, the bathers have formed a little crowd. I run towards them, I no longer recognize myself, everything happens as if I weren't myself but someone else, I am far away, I can no longer see the dog, only the two male nurses who hold my arms and legs. I see the dog suffering agony behind some steel bars and myself on

104

the other side of the bars, I am juggling with two oranges, but the dog doesn't see me, he is bounding away. I am holding the large stick, trying to tear it away. I can't. I hit the policeman, bite his fists. He lets go of the stick and I run towards the car with the dog, who does not resist but pulls me along.

An hour later a Civil Guard came to the front door of Fenosa's house—where I was staying. I made out certain words in Catalan: prison, insult to authority, foreigner. In this part of Catalonia, Fenosa is a sage, a kind of national monument. And so I was excused on the understanding that I left the next morning with the dog.

Mother turns towards me, but without seeing me, for she's asleep. It was she who used to watch over me when I was ill. I never knew any violence at home, not even verbal. Not even when I came home after having spent my first night with a man, although Father didn't like it.

I came home around five o'clock on the first morning train. That gave me two hours in which to recuperate a little before leaving again for the Lenin Library. I couldn't sleep. The eiderdown pulled up to my eyes, I listened to Xenia's and Vassia's muffled voices coming from the kitchen. Every morning Father ate cabbage soup. Mother watched him eat, then helped him get dressed. She put his watch on his wrist, she laced his shoes and she strapped on his arm. That morning they talked of me, trying to come to terms with the unprecedented event of my sleeping out. Father spoke loudest, but he did not shout. All this, he said, was Mother's fault! She answered him quietly: 'Liola is serious. She knows what she's doing.' Their habitual roles were reversed. Mother was the one who was always reprimanding me for little things, Father the one who defended me. 'Serious, serious!' Father growled, 'She knows nothing about life . . . She'll be hurt . . . '

But to me nothing was said, no reproach made. When Father kissed me before going off to work, I could feel how that morning he made a special effort not to hug me harder

106

than usual. The tiny breath of grace, the tiny breath between two words . . .

After Father's death I wrote a rambling letter to Mother in which I reminded her, among other things, of that kitchen where they both spoke in low voices after my first night spent away from home. I thanked them for being parents like that. Father died in the street while getting off a bus: Bus number 7, Kiev Station-Kuntsevo, the bus that Paul and I liked because it went by a little forest and stopped in front of wooden dashas. Stretched out in the snow, Father held in his only hand a string bag containing a large packet of buckwheat for making kasha, and a bouquet of mimosa. It was March 8th, Women's Day.

By the mere fact that he no longer sleeps with me, Paul makes me rediscover so much of my past. Including that night with Iouri, my first night spent with a man. I hadn't thought of it for years, yet now it comes back to me vividly. It happened twenty years ago when I was slowly recovering from my first unhappy love affair, a platonic one. 'Always unhappy,' said Father, to whom I told everything. 'First love affairs are always unhappy. It's normal comrade, quite normal.' We had these conversations together, and we used to call them 'Talking about Life', as if it were the title of a radio programme. These conversations took place on one condition: Mother's absence. This condition guaranteed the second, which was the supply of vodka. We sat facing each other in the kitchen, Father poured himself little glasses, and I drank tea. So far as I was concerned, Mother was wrong about only one thing. Right up to the end she scolded Father, if she so much as saw a glass in his hand. I told her this, but there was nothing to be done.

As soon as Father came back from the front, I understood once and for all that he needed vodka and he needed the company that goes with drinking it: the company of the clown Salomon, or my own, or even the company of another woman. Mother, who was a fury to any of her rivals, certainly did not share this view. I once saw her break an umbrella over the head of a woman who had shown herself susceptible to Father's wooden arm and his new 'Tsarist' uniform made from the finest wool. As for me, I wasn't frightened. I was sure that Father, one-armed philanderer that he may have been, would never leave us. Just as I was sure that Paul, when he began to be haunted, would never leave me.

Paul did not have the same sort of confidence when I told him that I was intrigued by an English author whom I had met at a friend's dinner—Paul never went out with me in the evening, for he had a horror of social occasions. He immediately started to hate everything English, and it was this that led him to his studies of Joan of Arc. He grew thin, he suffered from vertigo and pains in the heart, he started to drink Extra Dry Gin straight from the bottle.

I didn't know what to do to reassure him, I repainted the bedroom in pale pink, I wrote a novel for him in which a real enemy, a formidable one, the KGB, separated a man and a woman who resembled us a little.

I learnt my lesson: there is nothing worse than making those who are attached to you suffer. With my pink walls, my novel, I tried to tell Paul that we were inseparable. He looked at the room, he read the book and, as if he felt nothing, he simply said: 'It's beautiful. I don't know how you do it. It's really beautiful.' I was desperate. I hadn't left Paul. I had dreamed of my Englishman for a fortnight and then one morning I coldly drew a line through that dream, because I loved Paul. Five years later, Paul was to tell me, while putting his shoes back on: 'Everyone separates; everyone lives like that nowadays.'

The Lenin Library in Moscow doesn't close until ten in the evening. For me this is a sign of civilization. I was working on the ground floor, between two bookcases full of old books with green and gold bindings, next to a window which looked out onto the park—I had this special place as a favour from the very pretty woman librarian, who also made sure that I was not disturbed by the propositions of that strange race of bustling sex-starved men who, pursuing their mysterious occupations, haunt, as they do elsewhere, the public libraries of Russia. It was the beginning of term. Sun-tanned from Aunt Tanya's Scythian sun, I was all ready to throw myself into my course of German philosophy.

At ten on the September evening in question, I was queuing up to return a pile of books, my head a little dazed by what I had read about the Master-Slave dialectic. Suddenly I felt a pair of eyes on me. There are times when you feel a look as if it were heat or light, something altogether physical. And I felt this look at a very precise spot: where my neck meets my back.

I turn around. I see a figure dressed in beige, blond, a man. He doesn't smile. Nor do I. His eyes are grave. I am tired, or rather, hungry. I am thinking of the tomato juice I will drink in three minutes time at the Lenin Library tube station. I drink one there every evening, it stops me feeling hungry. He follows me to the exit and I am surprised to find myself not walking towards the station but beside him,

111

although he hasn't yet said a word. I keep pace with him, as if we were both subject to the same tropism, and at the same time, I discover a whole new district, a part of Moscow I didn't know. Every morning I pass by here, but I have never before ventured into these streets. A mistake, I tell myself, because I like these courtyards with trees and wooden benches, and the walls of the houses painted ochre, rose, indigo, and their double windows full of jamjars, cats, flowers.

Without a word, we walk a long way, perhaps three kilometres. We stop by a theatre which I recognize. In rather bedraggled costumes they perform plays by Lope de Vega. My friend, Iriana Pushkin, had a passion for this theatre and sometimes we went together. The door which my companion opens for me is just beside the theatre. We climb the stairs. The paint is peeling, and you can see all the colours that previously covered the wall: pink, white, green. The staircase is of old wood whose knots and grains look alive. I have never

112

before seen such a staircase. I will see others, years later, on the Left Bank in Paris.

Now I'm out of my element, and in a moment I'll be even more so when we go into a large well-proportioned room where there are bare beams, a fireplace, a large bed covered with a patchwork quilt and, in front of it, a wooden country bench. The young man turns every light on one by one, and disappears. Everything is new to me here. I pass my hand over the patchwork quilt and I tell myself out loud, that it is here and nowhere else that I shall lose my virginity. I have an account to settle with this virginity. For over a year it has made me feel like an invalid.

He was tall I think, with something slightly feminine about him, perhaps as a result of his blond hair; he had a long face which made him look serious. He seemed so inexperienced that I felt confident. In a glass on the bench in front of me were two white gladioli with short stems. I don't like gladioli, but these two looked very beautiful. And everything else too, the silence of the room, the gestures with

113

which Iouri poured out the Hungarian wine, gliding graceful gestures.

Silently we drink and the wine makes me hungry. Without my saying anything, he gets up and brings back bread, butter, cheese. He cuts the cheese and I notice his long fingers. He does everything nonchalantly, as if it had nothing to do with him. Again he disappears, and comes back with two hardboiled eggs. I can't eat these eggs, but they win me over completely: the final gesture of the first Act in his theatre of silence. In order to survive, one has to forget . . . Yet this doesn't prevent me from recalling and remembering intensely those eggs I never touched.

I got to know only a little about him, except the gentleness, both affectionate and sure, of all his gestures when he understood that it was the first time for me. He told me that his mother was an actress, and that he was finishing his studies at the Literary Institute. He accompanied me to the station on foot. I said I had no telephone, which was true. He gave me his number and I wrote it down with a pencil. 'I'll call you,' I told him, knowing that I never would.

Ten months later I met Paul at Ostankino. And I became his wife. I woke up beside him thousands of times. He would make me black coffee; he would come in and go out of the bedroom, his face covered in shaving soap; he would lean against the radiator and tell me, in his special way, what was going on in the world. He had the gift of making me laugh. In his views, he was like no one else. Each in our solitude, we lived side by side. By this I mean that we shared a great deal without this sharing becoming heavy, without ever swallowing each other up, without having the impression that we owed each other anything. When Paul was anxious, I never reproached him. I let the mood pass, and stayed there by his side. Paul called this 'a certain quality of absence'. I was simply trying to give him my confidence, my optimism. I have this optimism because I grew up in a country unlike other countries, and I grew up between Vassia and Xenia who knew so well how to love me.

I too, of course, was capable of being suspicious. Women, including some very beautiful ones, had their eyes on Paul, and it turned out that all the women he had loved before me were equally striking.

Occasionally I was frightened. I say occasionally, because the fear came and went and I never dwelt on it. Paul's presence was made as if to my measure. I didn't want any more. More would have bothered me, prevented me from living my life. Paul and I had an understanding which lasted, and which nothing and nobody will ever be able to efface. We were lucky. Yet a day of reckoning can come.

The first step taken towards that day was mine. I had made Paul ill: an equilibrium had been destroyed. I believe in necessities, in facts which you can't get round, in cycles. Why, for example, after that first night with Iouri which could not have been better, did I know it would never be repeated? Convinced that he would try to see me again, I no longer went to the Lenin Library but registered at the University Library instead.

Months passed. There were endless essays to write and exams to take. I put Iouri out of my mind and threw myself into the winter syllabus; then one day I went back to the Lenin Library. It must have been close to the new year, because I can see myself in the smoking room with my friend Iriana and we were talking about New Year's Eve. I didn't see Iouri come in. He was still blond and beige, calm and quiet. He came up to me and he slapped my face. I felt his blow like a rape and I was filled with rage. Just as twenty years later, I was to feel raped by Paul telling me about how he was haunted.

I still carry with me Iouri's mystery and the violence of his gesture which was so unlike the gentleness of our night together. I am still grateful to him. I prolong the night we spent together by musing, by writing novels. To everybody, his method. My own way of living my part, of coming to terms with my destiny, of shaping my days a little, is to write.

In one of the issues of *Continent*, Volodia

117

Bukovsky talks of the *château* which never left him during his imprisonment. Thrown into solitary confinement, he began to put his *château* in order. In his mind's eye, he planned everything down to the smallest architectural detail, the volutes of the entrance gate, the drawing room fireplace. For a long while he could not bring himself to accept that certain trees in the park of the *château* had grown too old and would have to be cut down; then he hesitated over what trees he should plant in their place.

A KGB officer calls him in for a re-education session and Volodia, while letting the officer talk, puts the finishing touches to a large reception he is holding in his *château*. The oak logs are burning; he slowly opens the heavy carved doors and his friends come in. Which of his wines should he serve first?

I read this, dumbfounded by Bukovsky's prodigious gift for survival, by the marvellous absurdity of his resistance. I believe more and more strongly in the boon of fiction, on paper or in the mind.

118

Once I had a dog staying with me, more a ball of fur than a dog. She was called Kitty, and she belonged to a Russian Jewish family who were scattered all over the world. Kitty ate only one thing: leeks. In the market at Gif I bought a bundle of leeks for her. I also bought carrots, whiting, mandarins. I knew whom I was shopping for and so it was easy: for Kitty and for the friends whom I had invited to dinner. I could already see their faces round the table. Often I watch my friends eating and forget to eat myself. Mother used to do the same.

A few months before I left Russia, I was sent as a future professor of philosophy to lecture about questions of nutrition (in the light of recent Party decisions) to collective farm-workers. This was at the height of the Maize and Khrushchev epoch, when the Party was promising that we would easily overtake American dairy and meat production. In a church, long since transformed into a cultural club, I found myself before my audience, almost all of them women. I couldn't bring out a single word about the radiant meat and milk perspectives which stretched before them. I didn't have the courage, and in any case, they didn't want to listen. They had come to speak, I could feel it. I asked them to do so. First subject: men—there weren't any, this was hard, it meant that they, the women, had to do all the heavy work. Second subject: men, the few who were there drank from morning til night, at sowing time, at harvest time and between times.

One of the women invited me to sleep in her home. She prepared a meal of, as we say in Russia, 'that which God has sent us'. Sixty years after the Great October Revolution, God had sent four boiled potatoes, a sour cabbage and a strip of fatty bacon. Each time I go to the market at Gif and see all the bulging shopping bags, I see them through the eyes of my Russian woman on the collective farm. And I can't get over it, it's like a fairy tale.

Following Paul's departure, there was a period of ten to twelve weeks when any display of food horrified me. Pauline was growing, she needed to eat, but it was hard for me to buy her a cutlet. My woman from the collective farm couldn't help me. The poet Ossip Emilievitch who died in a camp couldn't help me, although he is a poet for whom I have almost the same feelings as for Xenia and Vassia. Ossip is my spiritual Vassia, and he used to ransack the camp rubbish bins searching for something to eat.

The beauty of leeks or cauliflowers meant nothing to me. Only oranges spoke to my heart, and when they did, my heart tightened. Was Paul any more real than the son of Alexander Levy? I imagined Pauline with two oranges in her satchel for Paul. Then I ran home and took a spoonful of Valerian syrup.

The blood plasma bottle is empty. Mother is still asleep, she does not move. Through the curtains, the sky is becoming blue. Perhaps death doesn't exist; perhaps it isn't sad. What is sad is to fall asleep when you have made ready for death and then wake up again. You're back in their clutches and they're

121

incapable of doing anything to make the world they've dragged you back to less fearful, and at the same time they are convinced they've done their duty. I'm not brave enough to want to see Mother wake up again. And anyway, I won't look right for her. It's very hot in the room but I have started shivering. It is time this night ended. I would like to see people waiting for a bus. I would like to see a village in the forest with its chimneys smoking. If things weren't like they are with Paul, my first impulse would be to go to the post office and send him an interminable telegram, one of those telegrams which say nothing, but which used to do Paul and me so much good. But I no longer know how to say nothing to Paul. I am growing more and more cold. I had better begin to tell myself a story. It happens that sometimes I come across Pauline sitting very straight in a chair, not moving, silent, her eyes fixed. 'What on earth are you doing?' I ask her. 'Shush!' she answers, 'I'm telling myself a story.'

In the flat in Zelenograd I read a story by

Andrei Platonov—the story of Nikita. The son of a carpenter and a carpenter himself, Nikita comes back to his village at the end of the Civil War. He's still young, his mother is dead, his father is still alive, but his strength is failing. On the road, Nikita meets Liouba whom he knew as a little girl when they both went to school. Liouba's mother, who was a schoolteacher, is dead too. Nikita remembers her house, his father sometimes went there to repair some pieces of furniture. All their fine furniture was sold. Liouba has changed a lot, she's studying medicine in the local town and she reads heavy scholarly books. Nikita sees how she reads these books by the firelight from the half-open stove, how she has a thin neck and pointed knees, how she never eats enough. From the factory canteen where he works, he brings her boiled fish, kasha, bread. He also gathers wood for her stove. The spring comes. Liouba is still reading and Nikita doesn't know what to say to her; she, the cleverer one, tells him that he should marry. He marries her.

123

The old father's strength comes back to him. He makes them a bed, a wardrobe, but above all he concentrates on making a cot, a child's table, a child's chair. The seasons come and go. Nikita is not able to do to Liouba what a man does to his wife. Liouba is patient and still full of hope. But for Nikita, life has become a nightmare. Platonov doesn't say that he has a nervous breakdown, that's not Platonov's style, but it's like that. Throwing himself into the river would have been a happy end for Nikita.

He doesn't throw himself into the river. Instead he follows a beggar out of the village, ends up in the local town and there gets a job as a cleaner in the market. He no longer speaks at all, people believe that he is deaf and dumb and leave him alone. One day he encounters his father who has come to buy some tools. 'Liouba?' Nikita asks, pronouncing his first word for months. Liouba, his father tells him, threw herself into the river, was fished out, and now she spits blood. The father brings his son back to the village. And

124

now, on the very first night, Nikita makes love to his wife. But this does not stop Liouba from spitting blood. When Platonov wrote his story, there were no antibiotics.

I have no watch. I forgot my cigarettes downstairs in the cloakroom. I now dread waking Mother up.

A man in a white coat has opened the door: it is Vladimir Petrovitch who, this morning, told me what Mother's tumour looks like by showing me his clenched fist.

I get up and follow him into the hall with its green linoleum and shining white walls. We go into a room less heated than Mother's. There is an open window. The atmosphere is smoky. My head is turning a little. As if through a fog, I notice a bad reproduction of a Matisse, a little desk cluttered with papers, a steaming electric kettle, two glasses and a bottle of whiskey—the one I gave to Vladimir Petrovitch this morning. On a little table a lamp, covered with white muslin, gives off a soft light. The Russians have this habit of enveloping lamps in cloths or shawls.

Vladimir Petrovitch pushes a chair towards me and himself sits sideways on another. He takes a rather battered packet of cigarettes out of his pocket. Small Smoke, they're called. I recognize them. They're the Moscow equivalent of Gauloises and not bad. I try to recall the title of that painting by Matisse. Silence of a house? The house where silence lives? The silence of an inhabited house? Vladimir Petrovitch pours me out some very strong tea and hands me a cigarette and some matches, without formality, as if to another man.

'What time is it?'

'Six-thirty,' he answers.

'Yesterday you told me about a patient whom you were staying the night for. How is he?'

'He died. Twenty minutes ago,' Vladimir Petrovitch says this in the strictly professional tone I have already heard him use. He opens the whiskey bottle and pours some into his tea.

'Would you like some?'

'No. It won't do you any good either, drinking like this at dawn.'

'This morning, nothing does me any good.'

He is certainly younger than I. One gets worn out more quickly in this country. His hair hasn't been cut in Paris, but in one of a thousand barber shops where they shear your whole head in one fell swoop, with no scruples. He is very tall, very stooped, his eyes are bloodshot, his shirt stained.

'How long do you think Mother can hold out?'

'A month at the most. At her stage, there isn't usually far to go, but the old are sometimes surprising.' He pours himself some more whiskey, and, as if absent-mindedly, pours some into my tea as well.

'There's a lot of dying in your ward?'

'That's all there is. It's the corridor of the condemned. This morning I opened up one of them and closed him up again immediately. I killed him, if you like. Thirty-eight years old. A painter. A friend of mine. There was

127

nothing left to do. Two lungs gone, the trachea. You are from Paris?'

'No, it's my daughter who is from Paris.'

'How old is she?'

'Eleven.'

'After I saw you this morning, I told Pavlik, I've met a Parisian woman.'

Vladimir Petrovitch rummages through his papers and finds what he is looking for.

'Look. This is his last gouache, the painter's. What's your first name?'

'Liola.'

'Like my grandmother.' He smiled, just a little.

'Smiling suits you,' I said, looking at the gouache.

The painting is of a staircase. Somehow the way it is drawn emphasizes its steepness. The staircase stops dead and the light, visible on the wall beside it, makes one feel that the air is foul, unbreathable. I push this image away from me and resent it.

'No, don't cry. One shouldn't cry.'

'Was I crying?' I wasn't aware of it.

'Ah yes,' Vladimir Petrovitch says, he isn't a liar and to prove it he passes a finger under my eyes with a medical gesture. Suddenly everything snaps in me, falls apart, starts to tremble. Vladimir Petrovitch picks me up, puts me on his lap and presses my head against his shoulder. How long am I there, my arms around his neck? I don't know, time enough to calm down and to rediscover the courage necessary to return to Mother in her room. They must have increased the dose of her drugs, she's more absent than ever and doesn't speak at all.

It appears that on waking, she made signs to have the flowers taken away from her bedside, I don't tell her that I'm leaving, that my visa expires tonight, that Pauline is expecting me in Paris this evening. I say to myself, 'You are looking at your mother and you are looking at her for the last time.' In the corridor outside, one of the women who shares Mother's room comes up to me and tries to comfort me. She's kind, courageous. I look at her, remembering Vladimir Petrovitch's phrase: the corridor of

129

the condemned. I embrace her, wish her a good recovery and go downstairs.

Kostia is waiting below. The entrance hall is empty. In the cloakroom, a large lady in a white blouse grumbles at me, in fact scolds me, because the little loop on the inside of my coat collar is unsewn; she couldn't hang my coat up on the peg, she says. Her sharp abuse shakes me up and brings me back to life. Ever since I was little, I've been told off by cloakroom attendants, in the Lenin Library, in the opera, in cafés, everywhere, always because the little loop on my coat collar has been missing or unsewn. I smile. A little more and I'll be laughing outright. The attendant calms down. She thinks perhaps I'm mad.

Driving in Kostia's car, I notice for the first time the colossal statue of Lenin standing on the Zelenograd central square. I hadn't noticed before, there were other things on my mind. It is so large and its pedestal is so high that even if you knew it was there, you'd have to screw your neck and deliberately look up to

130

see it. At the same time I see, on a nearby roof, some large neon letters which spell out: 'A newspaper not only makes propaganda for the masses, it activates them.' Signed Lenin.

'You have understood,' says Kostia, 'not only buggers you up with propaganda, but activates you as well. How right they are to insist upon that! We run about, we get bored, we drink, we kick the bucket, and we would be quite capable of forgetting what a newspaper really does. You might just remember that a newspaper buggers the masses with propaganda, but that isn't all! Then you lift up your head to see what the weather looks like, and what you've forgotten comes back to you: A newspaper fucks the masses into activity!'

Kostia is wearing his steel-rimmed spectacles, which we bought together on the Boulevard des Italiens. They are the sort of glasses that nineteenth century revolutionaries wore. He drives perfectly well, but on the road back to Moscow we are stopped three times.

When the police stop a car, the driver is obliged to get out to show his papers. They don't look at the papers, they simply sniff the driver's breath. It's a control without any violence involved, but it's boorish and insulting.

'Can't one protest?'

'It would do no good,' says Kostia, 'but, of course, they'd do better to stop that lorry there!'

I screw up my short-sighted eyes to see the lorry better. A marvel. Huge, broken down, patched up, as if home-made from old wardrobes and plumbing, and on top of this lorry a large wooden chest tied with a rope whose end is whirling round in the air like a lasso, and the lorry is going at top speed, charging along the icy road, in fact, it's not charging, it is flying, it is dancing like death. It spins round, it slips sideways, it continues on the wrong side of the road. Kostia hasn't slowed down, he too is charging after this mad lorry. I start to scream. I no longer know where I am, there is an avalanche of icicles, sunflowers, tombstones, saucers, oranges. 'Kostia,' I scream, 'I'm frightened! Overtake him, overtake him.'

My screams wake me up. Is it that I still want to live?